Love's Sweet End

Candy Marie

authorHOUSE®

AuthorHouse™
1663 Liberty Drive
Bloomington, IN 47403
www.authorhouse.com
Phone: 833-262-8899

Published by AuthorHouse 10/26/2020

ISBN: 978-1-6655-0543-7 (sc)
ISBN: 978-1-6655-0542-0 (e)

Library of Congress Control Number: 2020920965

Print information available on the last page.

Contents

Preface

In everyone's life there are always regrets. For me, it's that one epic love that burned not only in my memory but deep within my soul as well. That one young man that would come to mind late at night; of days gone by, as I lay in bed trying to sleep. The one name that could stop me in my tracks and without fail, make my heart race. The one person that I regret leaving behind to this day. Whose heart I have, for the last fifty years, not forgiven myself for breaking. It was the poorest decision I ever made concerning the one man who loved me with all his heart and soul. But out of fear, I ran. He would prove to be the last man that would love me in that way. His name; Chip Lowery. However, fate was not finished with us....yet.

Acknowledgements

I want to thank my editor and friend Clyde Aly and his "red" pen that he used so freely; for his many hours of correcting and editing. It was he that convinced me to write this love story of us in the first place. I'm thankful for my friend Brenda Ray and my sister Mary Lindeman for the time they put into reading the story and offering their critique. Thank you for helping me with the story's ending. Thank you Paul Lindeman for taking the time to use your professional graphic talents in order to create a beautiful cover that fits the story to a tee. I want to thank my husband Joe Grossi for his infinite patience as I painstakingly wrote this story based on my life and 1st love while collaborating with Clyde.

It indeed takes a village to create something that is beautifully worth while. No one is an island.

Chapter 1
Reflections

I ALWAYS LOVED WALKING THE PROPERTY that Terry and I purchased three years prior in 2019. I especially enjoyed the walks early in the morning just after sunrise. Before Terry passed, we had created a walking path and placed benches throughout. This morning there was a slight summer breeze blowing through the trees. I stepped up my pace as I walked to my favorite spot on the property. It was the garden patch of yellow and orange Day Lilies that I had planted when Terry and I first moved there. The house was finally complete with my big front porch. The porch was my favorite place to drink my morning coffee and watch the sun rise.

I had a spring in my step. It had been only one month since Terry passed away and today I was flying to finally meet Chip in Dallas, Texas. Forty seven years since that fateful morning in Port Lavaca when he left me. Seemed like forever since I had seen him last until he surprised me; showing up at my house that evening in March.

My heart had gained a new life of it's own. Joy filled me with the anticipation of finally putting my arms around the one man that I had been in love with since I was seventeen. How I had longed for Chip!

I boarded the plane and took my seat by the window, flying on air. Finally, after all these years, going to Texas to marry my Chip. I couldn't help but think back over my life. With all that had taken place, with every delay and detour, our undying love remained. It lay just under the surface buried deep within my heart. He had refused to see the love and that thread of connection between us being the analytical man that he was. Yet that thread between us remained strong.

As years went by, I had successfully, or so I thought, put away my memories of him. I chalked it up to another failure and finally moved on. I never liked to think about our time together because of the pain and regret that followed. I fought many times through the years against the deep longing to see him again or wishing that he were next to me in the night; holding me. I had hoped against hope that one day we would meet again and I could make things right. Chip never knew how I really felt.

I was twenty two living in Port Lavaca when he came to see me. My mother had given him my phone number and we had spoken quite frequently for two weeks as we did when we first met. He asked if he could come see me. He had an interview for a job in Corpus Cristi and wanted to stop by. It was March of 1977. I was newly divorced for a second time. Working midnights at Circle K and as a reserve officer for Calhoun County's sheriffs department left little time for anything else. I had hardened my heart against men in general. I already convinced myself that I was over Chip. So I continued to move on from one failure to another. Then one day, the phone rang. It was Chip.

"Sarah, this is Chip Lowery. Do you remember me?" He asked. " Your mother gave me your number."

My heart raced. "Yea, of course!" What a stupid question to ask me I thought. How could I forget? "How are you doing Chip?" The sound of his voice caught me completely off guard. I wish mother had warned me.

"Your mother told me that you had gotten divorced. I wanted to see how you were doing." Chip said.

"I'm ok. Just staying busy working two jobs. I pull all nighters at Circle K and work part time at the sheriffs department here in Calhoun County working mostly radio calls. Sometimes I go on ride alongs. How are you?" I asked.

"I'm doing good." Chip replied and we talked for awhile.

He continued to call daily and we would talk for long periods of time. It was as if we had never stopped.

One evening he called; but this call was different. He sounded like he was a man on a mission.

"Hi! Good to hear from you. How are you?" I asked.

"I'm fine. Look, would it be okay if I came down to Port Lavaca to see you? Chip said.

"Sure." I replied. "What's up?"

"I want to talk to you; to see you face to face." Chip said.

"Okay, come on. I work nights but you can sleep here and we can talk when I get home in the morning."

Chip said; " Sounds good. Hey, I have an interview in Corpus Christi. You want to ride with me?" He asked.

"Sounds like fun. Sure!" I answered.

I paused for a minute; wondering if I could handle seeing him face to face. But my longing to see him again over ruled my sense of dread. What could he possibly want to talk to me about? How do I handle seeing him again? Is it good or bad? This can't be good; I thought.

"Okay. See you soon." said Chip.

With that, we hung up. I wondered what he wanted. Why was he coming all the way from Odessa to see me? I continued on with my day, trying to sleep because I had to work that night. Needless to say, sleep eluded me for the most part wondering, "What does Chip want?" My stomach churned as I tossed and turned on my bed. When he arrived I would soon have my answer.

Chip arrived and stood at the door knocking. His smile was a sight for sore eyes. He stayed the night on the couch while I worked. Part of me wanted to call out sick from work. But I was the only one working that shift. So, I went ahead and worked all night. When I returned home the next morning, he was already up and ready to talk. I hated him being near me. I couldn't protect my heart against him. Memories and regret filled my head as he began to speak.

"Sarah, I wanted to tell you in person that I'm getting married next month. I decided on the way down here to marry the girl I've been dating for the past two years." Chip said.

My heart sank.

"Well… that's great Chip. I'm happy for you." I lied with a smile. "Why are you here then?" I quipped. I fought back my tears with inner anger. How could he do this after he had said that he would always love me? I was torn between feeling totally rejected and angry that he came. This was hard. He couldn't see that as my face hardened into a fake smile. I thought he knew me! But I continued to hold it together for my own pride's sake. The only way I knew how to do that was to place him in the same category as I had all the other men; users and liars. Right, wrong, or indifferent....that's the best I could do so as not to break down in front of him. How humiliating that would have been!

From that moment on, I didn't really hear another word that Chip said. My autopilot was on full throttle. It was the only way I was going to get through the remainder of his visit. I kept my sentences short and on point; all the while hiding my true heartbreak from him. After talking, we decided that it would be better if I didn't go with him to Corpus Cristi since it might offend the other woman he chose.

As he left, I smiled and waved goodbye. I played the game well. Chip never knew that he had been holding my heart in his hand for the last four years. Nor did he realize that he had just unknowingly tossed my bloody heart onto the floor and crushed it into a million pieces. I knew I deserved it. He never knew how his words cut me deeply like a sharp bladed knife nor of the many tears I cried as soon as he drove out of sight. It was truly over now. I felt empty. The reality of not being loved by him anymore was devastating. Chip would never know how desperately I needed him.

I consoled my heartbreak as I opened a bottle of wine, "At least he'll be happy. Chip deserved some happiness. He's really a good man;" I thought. Emotionally, I was a hot mess; in no shape to lay my heart bare to anyone from that time on in my life. Until Chip showed up at my door, I had numbed myself towards men in general. It was easy. They were all users. They all lied. But with Chip, I couldn't hide my own heart from myself. I suddenly felt like a lost cause; not fit for anyone. I told myself, "It's gonna be okay. You'll survive this too. You're not alone. God still loves ya." I sort of chuckled. But it sure felt the opposite as I grieved deeply, the reality that Chip no longer loved me.

By my third glass of wine I began to wonder if there was anything that I could have done to change his mind? What if I had thrown my arms around him and told him the truth? If he had known that I loved him still, would Chip had even wanted me? By this time I was indeed tainted. I had no one to blame for the horrific heartbreak that I felt but myself. I asked Chip in a later conversation if he had known that I loved him still would it have made a difference. He said no.

With my heart and soul shattering, I phoned my mother crying. Although she felt my pain as I wept, the only words that she could offer was, "I'm sorry too, Sarah Marie, that you're hurting. There's nothing you can do about it now but move on. Your pain will get less and less as time goes by. Believe me Sarah. It will get better with time." She lied. She loved my father to her dying day.

I knew mother was feeling pain too. She wanted Chip as her son in law. I blew it and she wasn't very happy with me. However, she was right. In time I grew colder and colder. Love was a joke to me.

Fear ran me in those days like a bitted race horse. I continued to numb myself to any good feeling and my heart turned black. I wanted to be hard and cold hearted. It was my only protection I thought; to help me live with my poor decisions, consequences and the childhood memories that haunted me still. The shaded memories refused to give me peace or let me go. My nightmares from childhood had returned again. Now and then a random thought would run quickly through my mind. Stupid Sarah! You let him walk out that door. You never told him that you even loved him. It became just one more thing to add to my list of foolish decisions.

After some time, the memories were successfully locked away and forgotten. The pain had been so devastating that my mind completely blocked out his visit. Pandora's box was securely bolted shut; never to be opened again; or so I believed. Months passed. Our sheriff lost the election and for my birthday, the new sheriff fired our whole staff.

One night on my way to work at Circle K, a man grabbed me from the bushes and dragged me into his house with hopes of raping me. He out weighed me by 200 pounds. I remember calling out Jesus's name; screaming for help as he ripped my blouse. The next thing I remember is being on the front porch and running like crazy for the store six blocks away. Texas held no good memories for me; so I returned home to Georgia.

Chapter 2
A New Start

$\mathcal{I}$N MAY OF 1978, I began a new job with the Coca Cola Company in Atlanta as a security officer. In 1981, I was offered a job in telecommunications which would have pushed my career forward in a very prestigious department of Coca Cola.

Instead, I chose to remarry for a third time and eventually had three children. I loved my life. Being a mother gave me purpose. I didn't feel alone anymore in this world. I loved my husband. With the birth of my first child, my heart unequivocally flew open. I was free for the first time since Chip, to truly love another human being. I adored my children and my husband; Camp. God chose to heal me during this time of some old childhood wounds. I had finally made peace with most of the past. The nightmares had vanished in light of truth. I was really free.

My mother died; committing suicide in January 1985. Camp and I traveled to Abilene, Texas to make the final arrangements for burying her. As Camp and I walked into the funeral home, there was that overpowering scent of flowers; the strong stench of the carnations was overwhelming. As the funeral director greeted Camp and me, I asked to see my mother's body alone. The director informed me that mother's friend and hairdresser Dotty had come as a last act of love for mother to fixed her hair and makeup. Walking into the room where mother's body lay, I was amazed at how beautiful she looked. Her hair and makeup, both done to perfection. The most amazing thing to me was her face. It was completely void of lines and wrinkles. She looked twenty years younger. Her body was completely at rest. Mother's body was peaceful. I hadn't seen her look that beautiful or restful in years.

As I stood there I recalled the last time that we spoke on the phone. She was still in the hospital. I told her that I loved her at the end of our conversation. Her last words to me were, "Do you really love me Sarah Marie?" It broke my heart that she would have to ask me such a question.

"Mother, of course I do. I do love you! Please don't ever doubt my love for you!" I emphatically replied. My heart ached.

The next time that I phoned her she was at home and she refused to speak to me. I knew something was wrong. A few days later on January 25th, she took her life.

As I thought back to the last conversation, I softly whispered into her ear, I love you. Then gently kissed her cheek and wept as I held her hand for the last time. It took death to bring peace to her body. My only hope was that her soul found rest as well.

Visitation began that evening. I remember quickly looking down the page of the opened visitation book at the funeral home. I was curious to see who had come by for the viewing. I specifically sought one name; Chip Lowery. But it wasn't there. At the funeral I had secretly hoped to see him. But he never showed. I took a deep breath and walked away from the gravesite thinking it was probably for the best. Chip would say later that he was a bit miffed to only find out about mother's death two weeks after the fact. He would have come; if only to see me. Timing is everything. Ours seemed to be hit and miss.

In 1985 Camp moved our family to a small place outside of Jasper, Georgia. The marriage was becoming more and more difficult. I fought disrespect daily and a lack of love. I struggled to keep my marriage together. Going to counselors would at least fix me I thought. Maybe then Camp would love and respect me. Camp would never go with me to counseling. So, I went on my own. It didn't work for our marriage but it did help me to understand more of who I was and why I thought the way that I did.

In 1991, our family traveled as missionaries; making our home in Guatemala.

In 1998, Chip had taken a freelance job in Atlanta and searched for me while there; to no avail. I was in Florida. We were both married, so why he looked for me, I may never know. But deep inside his heart, I believe he missed me. I'm pretty sure about that.

Our family also lived for three months in Israel August through October, in 2000, working for the International Christian Embassy of Jerusalem. But November of 2000 is when my heart change forever. After nineteen and a half years of marriage, a nineteen year old Guatemalan woman named Nissa came unexpectedly into our lives. Camp had emotionally attached himself to her while attending the annual assembly of churches previously in November of 1999. He had assured me that she was thirteen and that he just wanted to be a father figure to her. He was nicer to that girl than to our own daughters. We fought bitterly over that many times.

By late spring of 2000 I found out that she was not thirteen; but nineteen years old. The arguments continued into the fall. After many heated arguments, I gave him an ultimatum that he say goodbye to her on his next trip or we were through. He took the trip to Guatemala where Nissa lived in November of 2000 for the annual assembly of churches. I wondered who he would choose. Upon his return, Camp and I drove to the drugstore in Bonita Springs, Florida where we had moved to be near his stateside mission. As he parked, Camp turned to me and said calmly; "I know that you're dying to ask me what happened? What I decided."

"Okay Camp. What happened in Guatemala with Nissa? Did you say goodbye?" I inquired.

His reply? " No, but I distanced myself from her."

Looking straight at him I asked, " Why didn't you say goodbye? I told you that it was either me or her?" I began getting upset. But what he said next had never entered my thoughts.

Camp looked me and blatantly said; "I didn't want to crush her heart."

With tears in my eyes I said, "Camp, I've served you for almost twenty years. I've let you take my inheritance and pick out that small ugly house that we lived in out in the middle of nowhere..." I began to yell at Camp. "I followed you to to Florida. I HATE FLORIDA! I NEVER WANTED TO MOVE TO GUATEMALA BUT I WENT!! You have spent most of our marriage restricting me from my Jewish friends and congregation, and EVEN MY MESSIANIC PRAISE MUSIC JUST BECAUSE THEY SANG IN HEBREW!!! My arms and hands hysterically flying through the air in a fit of rage, I continued screaming at him.

"You say you're not in love with her! You're not having an affair and... NISSA IS STILL MORE IMPORTANT THAN ME?" HER FEELINGS RATE HIGHER THAN MINE?" I wept uncontrollably. We drove home in silence as I toughened up that night and closed my heart to him forever.

In that one fateful night after almost twenty years of marriage I gave up. I still remember the sudden rip inside my heart and soul as it tore in two. My world once again, had fallen apart; leaving nothing left inside but shock and the realization that I was not important to him at all. My life's desire to have a happy family and to be truly loved was shattered. That night in my heart, I divorced Camp. I emotionally closed down. The final nail in the coffin came the next day when a girl from the mission trip came over to our house. She had photos to show me that had been taken on the trip in Guatemala. One was of Camp and Nissa cheek to cheek in a church. That was it. He lied.

After she left, we fought bitterly again outside. Camp hated being called a liar; but that's exactly what my take on the whole horrific situation was. He lied. Even with all that reality slapping me in the face, I tried making concessions. I offered to move back to Guatemala if he would just stay away from the church she attended. He refused. I then threatened him with divorce if he didn't resign and leave the mission; moving us back to Georgia. After three days of deliberation, Camp agreed to my terms. We did move back. Resentment filled Camp's soul and he despised me in his heart for making him resign as Vice President of the mission. With my heart broken, the trust was long gone. It took three more years of counseling and ugly truths spilling out before the divorce became a legal reality. The emptiness and the longing for someone, anyone to show me that I mattered grew stronger. I was angry with God and man. I moved out and never looked back.

In February of 2005 I turned fifty years old and once again alone. I phoned my best friend Jenny, who lived in Baltimore, Maryland one day and said, "Girl, we've both had one hell of a bad year. Let's take our Visa credit cards and celebrate my birthday in the Bahamas." I laughed. At first I thought...this is crazy! I already work three jobs and I can barely make my bills. But I was a half a century old and needed something fun to do. I told Jenny, "Let's do it! Why not?" So off we went on a three day cruise to the Bahamas. That three days is still a blur except to say.... I dance and drank and dance some more. It took a week to get over the three days that we partied hardy.

It was that same year that Chip had another job in Atlanta and wanted to look me up to see how I was doing. He changed his mind however because he was married. Although married, apparently I had never left his heart or thoughts it seemed.

I continued to go to church on Sundays. I even read my Bible. But talking to God in those days didn't come easy. How do you talk to someone with your need for healing when He didn't answer your prayers for your marriage? Right or wrong, I was so disappointed in Him. But as humans, we have the right to choose right from wrong. God would have broken His own laws had He made Camp choose me. Still, it was a hard pill for me to swallow and to speak to The Lord about anything deep.

In the fall of 2005, I was in service one Sunday morning when an American missionary moving to Guatemala came to speak at our church. I had heard it all before as he sang the praises of what God had called him to. He had a wife and she was with him there. Yet, it was all about him. As he began, I could feel anger welling up within me. I always sat on the back row just in case I needed to make a quick escape from too much reality. I cried a lot in those days privately.

The Lord spoke to me while that missionary was speaking and showed me in a vision what my soul looked like. If the reader chose to look up photos of Hiroshima, Japan after the A bomb, they would see exactly what I saw in my vision. I was horrified at the sight. The Holy Spirit was digging into a buried grave. I felt the unbridled grief coming to the surface. Panicked, I quickly ran outside into the parking lot. I screamed as loud as I could. " I was a good wife! I tried! You did nothing to stop him!" The pain rushed from the deepest recesses of my soul into the open and it was overwhelming. The agony of rejection was too much and I couldn't ignore or escape it any longer. I couldn't even drink it away. I was absolutely broken. Shattered dreams and empty promises had destroyed me.

The Lord began His gentle healing that day within me. The Holy Spirit that I had grieved so much spread out all through me. I felt His warmth and presence that day. I returned safely back in His arms. My heart was on the mend and most importantly, I finally began to have some peace within my soul with the Lord. I could actually look in the mirror and like the person reflected back at me.

2006 rolled around. It was a Sunday morning just before spring. A friend of mine at church came up to me. She had decided that I needed to have a godly man in my life.

"Choose any one of these men and I will introduce you to them." Macy said as she grabbed my wrist in a vice grip.

"Macy, I have just gotten in a good place with the Lord. I need a man godly or otherwise like a hole in my head. No!" I replied quietly.

But Macy was relentless. She dragged me around the vestibule by my wrist refusing to let go. It was so embarrassing.

"Pick one!" She insisted. Minutes passed. I continued to argue with her. Finally, just to get her to stop, I looked around and saw a man that was standing by his mother next to one of the windows. I pointed and said; "He might be good looking if he ever smiled." Immediately, Macy pulled me over to the man. He was about 5'9" with brown hair and a goatee and mustache. He had sad brown eyes. I somehow knew that he had a story of his own to tell.

Macy announced; "Terry, I want you to meet Sarah. Sarah, meet Terry. My job is done!" She exclaimed in victory as she finally turned me loose. We both politely said hello just as the music began. I turned and hurried into the sanctuary.

The next week I came into church bubbly as usual and Terry stood by the coffee table as I walked up for my second cup of coffee of the morning.

"Hi Sarah." Terry greeted me. "Needing coffee?"

I was surprised that he remembered my name. We spoke for a few minutes and Terry asked me out. He seemed to loosen up around me and even smiled. The stoic man that I met the previous week could smile! Who knew? The dates became more frequent and eventually, we married that same year. I loved him but there was a piece of my heart safely tucked away; waiting to see if there was another shoe to drop.

While dating, Terry was very attentive. He even remembered that I hated diamonds and roses of any color. he surprised me with my favorite flowers one day. He remembered that my favorite flowers were Tiger Lilies and surprised me with a beautiful bouquet of them. That impressed me. I told my ex husband for twenty years that I hated roses and yet, every anniversary I received red roses with one yellow rose to celebrate the year to come. Really? So, needless to say, Tiger Lilies caught my attention.

While on our honeymoon in the Smokies on our second day, I couldn't help but notice Terry's eyes wondering to every pair of younger legs in short shorts. My trust level went down. I finally called him on it.

"Terry! We're on our honeymoon and you have done nothing but stare at girls legs! Really?" I exclaimed.

"I'm sorry. But no matter how many I stare at, you're the one I'm going home with." He smiled.

If he thought that his statement brought me comfort, it did not. We continued to walk around. He wasn't as conspicuous about checking out other legs from there on. But the damage was done.

Life continued to happen over the next thirteen years. Family moved in; brought drama; and moved out. His mother moved in and for seven years I was her main care giver. She was a kind woman with many needs.

Terry and I both struggled to maintain our marriage in the midst of it all. There were more challenges than time allows to tell; while trying to be everything to everyone; it did not work. We were hardly ever alone. Little by little, Terry's attention grew less and less while his drinking and silence grew more and more. I failed miserably trying to please everyone who came and went at our house. In the end, no one was happy with the results; least of all, Terry. He became very dissatisfied with our situation. Family dramas and our savings dwindling to zero certainly didn't help either. It was hard. By 2017 he was fifty five and I was sixty two. His depression was hard to handle on a daily basis. We had, unfortunately, by summer, become nothing more than mere roommates. We didn't fight or argue. Terry didn't talk to me anymore. It was a very lonely life for us both.

Chapter 3
Two Worlds Collide

A VERY SUBTLE CHANGE WAS SWEEPING unnoticeably into my life. June 27, 2017, I was on Facebook when Messenger pinged. As I looked to see who it was, a familiar name appeared; Chip Lowery. My heart stopped for a moment. That name… I had not seen nor spoken that name out loud in years. I did nothing. I didn't know how to respond. Of course, I could have simply said hello. However, I chose to say nothing.

July 19, 2017: My phone pinged.

Chip texted. "What have you been up to."

I replied; "Not much. Just taking care of kids and trying to stay sane. How about you?"

Chip: "I've been on a job and just finished up. Filming was brutal today in the heat."

I texted; "LOL I bet. But you enjoy your work I'm sure."

Chip: "I would hope so. Been at it for over 40 years now. That's what I went to college for and it's why I took the job at the station. You remember KTXS?"

I chuckled. "Of course. Mother worked there and that's where I met you. What a silly question to ask me!"

"Yes it is; isn't it?" Chip texted. ☺ "I didn't know if you'd remember that or me."

"Chip, how could I forget? I've always been fond of you."

A moment of silence passed. Then he texted; "I've always been fond of you too."

I became nervous; realizing that I had probably said too much. I told Chip I had to go and left Messenger. I felt an old stir in my heart. So many years had passed but I remembered and it frightened me. I backed away and uninstalled Messenger for a time.

On October 11, 2017 Chip saw that I was on Messenger again and asked a simple question. "Did you guys make it through the hurricane unscathed?"

I didn't see his message until October 22nd. I decided to answer him this time.

"I'm sorry that I didn't answer. I had uninstalled Messenger for awhile." I didn't say why.

"Yes, we're fine. Just been busier than a one legged man in a butt kickin' contest. LOL" I Joked.

October 30, 2017

Chip replied to my message. "Why, after all these years, would I think that sounds like you? Glad to hear it. Central Texas is washing away. Abilene and here in Odessa are ok. But we haven't seen the sun in over a week."

I had begun searching for something pertinent to say to keep the conversation going.

"How is Cisco?" I asked.

"Cisco had rain but no flooding that I know of." Chip wrote.

Someone called me and I had to go. My mind told me something was up. I ignored the warning. If nothing else, Chip was back in my life as my Facebook friend.

November 3rd I wrote Chip back. "Thank you. My cousin Jesse lives in Cisco. But she called to check on me and she's ok. You know, my mother's birthday was yesterday."

"No I didn't know that." Chip replied. " I really liked your mom. She kinda took me under her wing when I started working there at the station. In fact, she knew my parents. Your grandmother knew my parents and me as a baby. They all went to the same church. Somehow I met your grandmother and she told me that."

"Do you go to church now?" I asked. "I know that you used to be agnostic."

I could tell I ruffled his feathers.

"Not agnostic. Just not practicing. Kinda in between churches right now. Was Catholic for years." he wrote.

"Gladys was her name. I remember now. Yes, BTW, seem to remember your birthday is Ground Hogs Day. Is that right?" he wrote.

"Yes it is; and I might add that I am always correct on weather. LOL I'm heading out. We go to early service." I said.

"Have a good evening. I'm at a wedding dance. So I will be awhile." Then Chip added; "Take care and stay in touch."

I was feeling elated deep inside. I wrote back. "Definitely!" 😊☐

I never heard much from Chip in 2018. We texted twice.

New Year's Day 2019 had been uneventful until I received Chip's message. "Happy New Year!"

I replied back the same. I heard nothing else until my birthday.

"Happy Birthday" 🎈🎊 Chip wrote.

I didn't see Chip's message until the next day.

February 3rd I saw his message and was eager to talk to him again. Chip remembered my birthday! I felt a tinge of excitement run through my whole body. Then, I thought...this is crazy. It's just me. Put a lock on it girl.

I replied to Chip's message. "Thank you Chip! Can't believe I'm 64! I don't feel 64." (Truth was, he brought out the girl I used to know and I was loving every minute of it.) It was as though I found a new breath easily flowing in me. New life in my otherwise challenging day to day existence. I was beginning to feel light hearted. I smiled more and giggled over silly things. What was wrong with me?

"Yeah, don't feel 64.... until I look in the mirror. 👀Mirrors are evil!😈LOL"

"Will you still need me? Will you still feed me, when I'm 64? Paul McCartney Beatles." Chip replied.

"Oh" 😂 "Take me back to the old days!" I laughed.

"Love those times!" He replied.

"That's very sweet of you to say." I replied.

And there it was ... Memories creeping out of my Pandora's box and back into my heart.

I began to be drawn in as though I was 17 again, by his wit and charm that apparently, he had perfected over the years. Chip was funny; like a breath of fresh air. I didn't even realize that I was pulled into him again. How I had missed him! That was all I felt.

I heard no more from him for months. I thought that he had gotten busy and had no time to talk. So, life went on.

July 7, 2019 I decided to reach out.

"Hey, are you all getting wet? The rain teases us here in Georgia. One or two drops here and there."

To my surprise, Chip wrote back.

"Pretty wet spring here. But the summer heat is setting in. I'm in Dallas on a job right now and it's so humid. But Odessa is dry heat. Guess you guys are used to humidity.

"Very!" I wrote. "Everyone fusses if I turn off the air when it's below 80*. I'm not a fan of air conditioning unless it gets above 85*. LOL"

"Yeah, I'm warm natured too but only when it's dry. I'm used to the west Texas desert. When we lived in El Paso it was so dry that we could still use swamp coolers." I didn't want to sound too ignorant so I just agreed. My real question was and is... What's a swamp cooler?

We messaged for almost an hour just texting about our lives. Chip told me that he had lost his wife in 2013 to cancer. He was with the same woman all those years. It had to break his heart to lose her.

I had skipped lunch to message with him. I finally had to eat something so I told Chip that I needed to go.

Chip replied; " Good to hear from you. Don't be a stranger!"

And there it was ......more memories seeping out.

From July through December of 2019 we hit each other up now and then just to say hi.

Chapter 4
Revealed Truths

THE NEW YEAR BROUGHT NEW revelations. On my birthday of 2020, Chip turned it up a notch. My birthday had been a dud all day. Terry had been ignoring me throughout the day and when I asked if he would spend time with me, got mad and yelled at me. Terry finally went to bed; leaving me alone.

The Super Bowl was that night and Chip and I messaged through the entire game on Facebook. It was so much fun and he really made my birthday evening a happy one; bantering back and forth over the game. I so enjoyed the much desired company and laughter! However, at one point, near the end of the 4th quarter, Chip ask me to switch to Messenger. So I did. Suddenly, the conversation got real.

Chip began talking about that day so long ago when I left him. He spoke of the pain he felt as he drove me to the airport. He said that he loved me so much it hurt. As he continued, to my utter amazement, my heart flew open and Pandora's box became unequivocally broken as the memories began flooding into my mind; opening my heart. I remembered the feelings of love that I'd had for Chip. The tears I shed when I left him the first time; the last time. All the regret flew in my face. Years of consequences, reminding me of the greatest loss of my life just because I ran away from him. Chip had believed all those years, that I left because I didn't love him. I had to tell him the truth! It hurt me to know that I had broken his heart.

"What?!" I said; "it couldn't have been farther from the truth! I didn't leave. I ran! What I felt was so deep; so real! It was so scary for a seventeen year old that I fled the state. I ran home to safety."

(The truth was, Chip was everything I had ever longed for. Yet, the fear of him tiring of me; leaving me heartbroken in the dust; and living with mother, was a nightmare that I couldn't fathom. But especially taking a chance on Chip; if he changed his mind, it would destroy me. I only wish now that I had stayed and taken the chance on "us".)

Chip was shocked when he heard me say that I secretly was in love with him even though I ran back to Atlanta.

"Sarah Marie, I would have come and gotten you from Atlanta if I had known! I almost did; as a matter of fact! I made it all the way to my grandparents's house in Louisiana. I wanted you with me that bad."

I took a deep breath. I felt my heart beat faster and faster as Chip spoke those words. So many beautiful memories ran through my mind. It suddenly didn't seem as though it was forty eight years ago. It felt like only yesterday. The love that I had locked away filled me inside through and through. Oh my God! The love is still here in my heart! I was still in love with Chip after all these years! I had to keep that to myself. I was married. More and more memories, like a movie, were playing out in my mind's eye as Chip continued to talk about his memories of us; his great love for me, and the shock he was feeling over the fact that I left Texas in love with him. I wanted to cry. I was absolutely overwhelmed as each memory played out before me. He seemed surprised that I remembered so much. Tears began to well up in my eyes as I thought back. "Yes Chip, I do remember....."

Chapter 5
Summer of '72

IT WAS THE SUMMER OF 1972. I was obligated every year to fly out to Texas for a visit with my mother for one week; sometimes two. I always dreaded it. The first night I could count on mother chasing her valium with vodka and orange juice. Then, with each drink, she would begin to say terrible things about my dad. But I drew the line when it came to my step mother; Mama Jo. Mama Jo had been the mother that my own mother couldn't be to me. So, an argument ensued every first night of our visit. My visits always included a call to my mom as I referred to Mama Jo, begging to let me come home. The next morning I could always count on Mother dragging me with her to her office at the T.V. Station just outside of Abilene. She was head continuity writer for KTXS TV. She wrote all the T. V. Commercials. Everyone loved her. She was brilliant and very good at her job of creating commercials.

This time mother had cooked up a plan. There was a young man that she wanted me to meet. I agreed to meet him for arguments' sake. I dressed up in a cute light green sleeveless mini dress with my heeled open toed white sandals and headed off to the station with Mother.

We arrived at the station. As we entered, I watched as the two men standing in the lobby drooled over my mother's quick swish back and forth as she walked into the hallway. She still had it going on. Men still panted. I had to admit that I wished that I was as pretty as she was. Mother was not only intelligent, but a very sexy woman as well. She was 5'3" with thick Auburn hair. Never a hair out of place of course. Her nails long and perfect with fiery red nail polish and that perfect figure;

34, 24, 36. Yeah, I knew that I was not even close to that standard. We walked into her office and she phoned this guy to come to her office so that she could introduce us. Honestly, I was embarrassed. I knew that she had encouraged him to ask me out. Chip walked in and I smiled politely as we were introduced.

"This is Chip Lowery. Chip, meet my daughter Sarah Marie." Mother said.

I hated being referred to as Sarah Marie. It was the name that I was always called when in trouble. Chip was about 5'9" with brown, somewhat wavy hair that curled a little around his ears. He had crystal clear blue eyes that were soft and kind in appearance. When he smiled it made me smile as well. He had a huge shy grin. His laugh was infectious. Chip seemed friendly enough. What I gathered the first time we met was, with Chip, what you saw was what you got. He sat down on Mother's couch. I was sitting in the chair on the side in front of mother's desk. We spoke a little. I rose up from my chair and walked by him. Chip's eyes followed me as I did. Frankly, It pleased me that he had noticed me. It made me smile. I actually quietly giggled as I passed by him. I don't remember why I rose up from my chair and walked across in front of him. It was most likely to see if he noticed me. It's was a girl thing.

Chip told me later that my presence filled the room. He called me vivacious. He was actually attracted to me. To my surprise, he wasn't the only one being drawn in. He finally found his chutzpah and nervously asked me out and I said yes. My eyes lit up and a huge smile appeared on my face. The butterflies were flying in my stomach. Neither one of us had a clue as to what would come of this one date.

Chip took me out to eat that same night. He and I talked about all sorts of things. We communicated so beautifully. I was very surprised that we sat for hours at the restaurant just talking and laughing as though we had known each other for years. He was so easy to talk to; so real. We just fit. I felt at home with him. How could that be? Chip was funny and his laugh, infectious. How I loved his laugh! Sometimes through our conversation I'd forget that he was five years older than me. I don't know if it was because I held a decent conversation on a number of subjects or he was less mature than I thought. I just knew that I could listen to him all night. He had me mesmerized. I even liked his Texas accent! His smile though, he had me with that big ole grin of his. There was so much more to Chip. He was like an onion. Except, he was a Vidalia onion; sweet and strong at the same time.

At the end of the night he walked me to the door and just gave me a peck on the cheek. My only thought after that was...How does he really kiss? After all, a kiss was and still is very important in my book! I could see in his eyes that he wanted to kiss me. Could he not see that I was saying yes? I found out later that Mother made him promise to be good to me. I knew exactly what that meant. "Thanks Mother." Talk about a mood spoiler! I came in and as I lay in bed that night, all I could think of was Chip. I adored him! It was crazy! I just met him! Yet, I felt like I had known him forever. I could hardly wait until the next day. I was definitely going to the station with mother! I was filled with anticipation of seeing Chip, hoping that he would ask me out again.

Chip would write later that he couldn't even describe how he felt after that first date. I was his Pixie. I liked being thought of as "his" Pixie. He wrote; "I just stood there watching the most beautiful girl who had ever liked me. She was so full of life and she actually liked me. I stood amazed. But she moved so fast that I couldn't keep up emotionally. I still can't."

That was sort of a funny statement to me; even now as I think about it. Hum.... I've never had a problem making up my mind as far as knowing what I wanted. Maybe that's what he meant.

The next morning I woke up and began to get ready. Putting on my makeup; standing next to mother, she watched me for a minute or two and began to grin. I caught that all familiar knowing grin in the mirror and looked back at her inquisitively. She said nothing. She just continued with that annoying grin and glanced my way now and then. A couple of minutes passed. I grew impatient with her.

"Okay, what?" I demanded. "What is that grin for?"

"You're going to the station with me? You don't like going to the station." By this time she had a huge smile on her face. "You tell me that you don't want to because it's boring."

"Just thought I'd spend time with you up there. That's all." I replied very matter of factly.

Mother giggled. "It wouldn't happen to have anything to do with a certain young man who works there; would it?"

I could feel myself blushing and unwittingly, I slightly grinned. "Stop it!" I angrily replied.

My face couldn't hide my elation with the anticipation of seeing Chip. Mother was definitely pleased. She was hoping her plan to keep me there in Abilene with her was working.

We finished getting ready and left for the T.V. station. As we arrived and walked through the front door, I began looking around to see if I could catch a glimpse of Chip. I waited in her office. Then went to the break room to refill her still half filled cup of coffee. Chip never came to her office. Surely he knows by now that I'm here, I thought. Mother saw the frustration on my face and decided to call back to the control room and asked if Chip was there.

As mother hung up the phone she said; "Sorry sweetie. He's off today."

I became like a female tiger in a cage; pacing around for the remainder of the day. With all the things that we had talked about the night before, he never once mentioned that he was off; that he wouldn't be here.

By the end of mother's work day I was just plain mad. I pouted; saying nothing all the way back to her apartment. What a waste of my day; I thought. How stupid of me to think he would be crazy about me after only one date. Then I was angry with myself for thinking more of myself than I should. Insecurity and fear ran my emotions as usual; and then a fleeting thought... "I don't care." I was seventeen and still had Brandon back in Georgia. I tried to console my disappointment but it wasn't working. I wondered why Chip wasn't at work. Why he hadn't told me was sort of baffling.

As we walked through the opened door of mother's apartment the phone was ringing. I quickly ran for the phone. It was Chip! He was calling to ask me out to a movie. My pouting turned rapidly into a smile from ear to ear. Mother was laughing at my girlish giggles as I ran for the bedroom to find the perfect outfit. My heart was beating so fast and hard that I had to stop for a moment to calm myself down. "Good grief," I thought. "Chip has drawing power over me. I can't already be hooked. I just can't! What's wrong with me?"

I found my two piece short set and decided to wear it. The top was a two toned brown and had short sleeves with a smart looking collar. I laid it out on the bed. I looked at the wall clock.

Just then, the female in me kicked in... I Screamed out;

"Dang nation!"

I was running out of time to freshen up or do anything with my hair. He would be there any minute. I quickly refreshed my makeup and brushed my hair. I couldn't believe how nervous I was.

Barely twenty minutes passed and there was a knock at the door. I tried not to appear so excited. But then our eyes met and I felt like ants were crawling just under my skin and all throughout my body. Oh, I had it bad. Looking into Chip's crystal blue eyes and seeing his smile took not only all the doldrums away of my boring day, but my breath as well. I might not have had him with me that day, but he was there and mine now! I had no plans of turning him loose easily that night.

Chip drove a beat up multicolor 1962 Chevy Impala Biscayne. As he opened the car door for me I noticed a big old fashion air conditioner that was sitting square in the middle of the front seat. At least that's what Chip said it was when I inquired as to the huge thing in his car. We could barely hold hands much less sit next to each other as he drove. We sort of laughed about it. I didn't care what kind of car he drove or what it looked like. Chip was all I wanted. He was my dream guy. Chip was the kind of guy every girl wishes for as her own. The best part was, Chip didn't see that in himself and that's what made him even more desirable to me. For me, he was perfect! He was manly but gentle.

Once at the theater, we found our seats. The movie began. "Clockwork Orange" was shocking to both of us. It was so foul and disgusting. Chip didn't look at me and I was so embarrassed that I didn't look his way either through the whole movie. He had brought me having no idea what the movie was about. At the end of two hours and twenty six minutes of this excruciating movie, we walked out in silence. He turned to me and finally apologized for choosing such a sleazy movie. It happens...

Even knowing Chip for such a short time, I knew that he would have never purposely taken me to such a movie. That just wasn't who he was.

As we arrived at his car, Chip said that he was freezing. It was a warm summer night; around 80*. A soft warm breeze blew. I thought how strange that he's cold. I looked at him for a moment and found the solution.

"Roll your sleeves down silly!" I then proceeded to take his sleeve and roll it down for him; buttoning his cuff. I repeated that with the other sleeve. "There." I smiled up at him. Chip realized and he would say later, that was the precise moment he realized he was hopelessly falling off a cliff in love with me. I still hadn't gotten that memo yet. I was still at the "wonder if he likes me stage" or "just being nice for mother's sake?"

Chip drove me back to my mother's apartment and walked me to the door. He leaned down and kissed me lightly. Then kissed me again. Wow… My lips were begging for more. I smiled up at him. But Chip decided that he needed to go. We said goodnight and after that, he just walked out. I closed the door quietly as to not awaken mother who was already asleep. I walked away. Suddenly, there was a light tap on the door. I quickly walked to the door and opened it. To my pleasant but somewhat puzzled surprise, there was Chip.

"What are you doing here?" I asked quietly.

"I wasn't ready to go home yet." He replied. A huge smile appeared on my face and he welcomed it. Chip stepped in and closed the door softly behind him.

Slowly, Chip bent down; touching my cheek and gently brushed his lips against mine. The ants began marching🐜🐜🐜 and electricity flashed throughout my body. My eyes were wide open as I gazed into his. Those blue eyes spoke volumes; so much love shining from them. For one brief moment I feared nothing. I knew that I was in over my head and all I wanted to do was drown in him. He lightly pressed his lips again against mine. Chip saw the sparkle in my eyes and could feel my heart pounding against his chest as He pulled me ever closer to him. For a moment, there was no doubt that I could have stayed in his arms forever! Then, without warning, Chip pulled away and looked deeply into my eyes. He seemed to be studying me. I saw the love. I felt it. Each time he kissed me, he was so gentle with me. But that was the calm before the storm.

I could feel myself falling deep under the weight of his spell. I had never experienced real love before. He was five years older than me. To me, he was a grown man. My heart and soul were hopelessly laid bare before him; and I knew at that moment, for the first time in my life, that a man held my whole heart in his hands. My soul felt one with his soul. I was powerless to resist. I was thoroughly captivated by his love as he began to hold me ever tighter against his body and kiss me. Each time, he paused, staring into my eyes and exposing my naked soul to his. Chip could read me. But I didn't care or feared nothing as he held me securely within his arms. His eyes were piercing me; drawing my heart out; joining his.

Suddenly, without warning, he drove his lips to mine; kissing me deeply. His lips covered mine perfectly as if his lips had been created especially to fit over mine. I had never been kissed with such passion! He grew stronger and stronger; pressing his whole body against mine; forcefully pinning me against the front door. I could feel his firmness against me and I was totally in his power. We felt each other's body and soul meld together perfectly. All I knew was that I never wanted him to let me go. Over and over he kissed me deeply; passionately. Each one mixed with such love and desire that I became one with his soul completely. His love seemed boundless. Chip wrote later that I became like sweet chocolate; melting into him. We fit and became one another's half. We couldn't get enough of each other. I needed him like I had never needed anyone before.

Then, just as suddenly as it began, he backed away from me; remembering his word to my mother. We were both breathless as we stared at each another for a moment. Chip slightly shook his head as if to get some clarity. With a smirk, he gave me a soft brush of his lips on mine. He turned quickly and said good night as he opened the door. I watched him as he walked to his car; leaving me limp as a dish rag and frustrated to my core. I was still breathless as I closed the door and fell backwards against it; closing my eyes. My fingers were lightly touching my lips; trying desperately to recapture his presence even if just for a moment. My body still trembled from the thought of his touch. All I wanted to do was scream "Come back!" But he was gone. I took a deep breath and walked into the bedroom to get ready for bed.

Sleep didn't come easily that night. Thoughts of him filled my mind; quickening my heartbeat and making my whole body quiver. I'd close my eyes; reliving the moments of our beautiful passion. ✳✳✳ The tingling had returned as I lay there in bed musing over the precious, yet all too short time with Chip that evening. I had never known a kiss like that before. I have never been kissed like that since. I knew that from that time on I would never be the same. My whole heart was his from that night forward. How could I possibly reconcile this craziness? At seventeen I knew I wanted Chip. Yet how could he even fit into my life? Could I really fit into his? He was in college. I was going into my Senior year of High School.

My fears began to speak. They kept getting louder and louder. Fear told me that he could hurt me and destroy my heart. He knew me. Oh my God….he did know me! He understood me and with him there was no pretense. My heart and soul had been laid bare before him. It frightened me. I was left with no protection. Chip had conquered my inner most being. Like the Trojan horse, this possible enemy was within my protective gates and my weapons that I had taken years to form, were now captured. I had lost control. He had conquered my heart. My next thought as I smiled slightly, I surrender. Take me. I'm yours. But then what? It was a hard night for sleeping; my thoughts wrestled with my sleep all night. Thank God; morning finally dawned.

The next day, Chip picked me up and took me with him to his garage apartment. He had some things he needed for work at the station. I walked in and sat on his bed. I remember crossing my legs playfully and swinging my lower leg gently back and forth in tempo with the music playing in my head as I watched him. He was aloof. I couldn't get his attention. He was purposefully ignoring me. We were all alone and I wanted him to come over to me and continue what we begun the night before. But… he continued to ignore me. I was not happy!

As soon as he gathered his things together, we left. I don't remember too much about that afternoon except that I was quieter than usual. I was mad! I was frustrated! I wanted him! Previously, I had not cared for sexual exploits. My childhood background threw cold water on anything others might have intended toward me sexually. Frankly, I was cold. Didn't mind kissing but anything else made me feel sick to my stomach and used. With Chip it was a different story; a whole new ballgame and I was ready to run the bases and slide into home.

"Sarah, get a grip on yourself girl. What is wrong with you?" I silently fussed as we drove off. My insecurities also began whispering to me saying, "He doesn't really want you. You imagined the love. He was only caught up in the passion of the moment. You know guys. Come on!" Fear set in as Chip drove silently to the station. I had contemplated staying longer but after his coldness, I now had doubts to whether I had experienced real love or just male passion the night before.

Chapter 6
Run Sarah Run

CHIP CALLED ME LATER AND asked if he could come over. He drove up that evening as mother was leaving for a night out. We gabbed as we sat on mother's sofa as if nothing had happened that day and I even enjoyed the conversation. Yet, with all the laughter, all the talk, Chip kept his distance and I was confused and wondered where I even stood with him. Every time he looked into my eyes I would question his motives as my fears raised their ugly head. Was he just there to keep me entertained for mother? Only time would tell which one would win out. It was nearing my time to leave. I didn't want to go. I wanted to stay; not with mother, but with Chip. Was he really my Chip? Did he really want me for himself?

How could we seemingly fit together so beautifully? How could it be that my heart felt so tied to his and that it appeared as if we had known each other for years instead of mere days? Nothing made sense. Everything screamed, " Stay, your home is finally found complete in his heart." Yet, my fears whispered as well. "You need to go. You're in a fairytale; not reality. You know how this will end!"

Suddenly he took my hand and pulled me close. I felt the warmth of his body as I scooted just under his arm. I turned to Chip and kissed him on the cheek; then smiled lovingly up at him. He grinned back and began to slowly kiss my face. Finally, what I had been waiting for... his kiss! No matter what, I could never forget the taste of Chip's kiss.

"Chip" I said sweetly, "I really care about you. I'm scared. I was not prepared to meet you and fall so" .... I hesitated for a moment. Chip looked intently into my eyes. His smile was no longer present. All I could think was, I've really blown it. Why did I have to say anything?

But he leaned in and gently kissed me again.

"Sarah," he confessed; "I'm in love with you. I don't want you to go. Stay awhile longer and let's see where this is going." I bit my lip nervously. "Please Sarah, give us a chance. You can finish school here. We can be together and get to know one another. Please stay."

I sat there for a moment and then threw my arms around him. He began to kiss me again. Just then, we heard the door open and it was mother with a strange man by her side. I began to bite my lip again as the man stepped into the living room. I could tell that she had been drinking. She smiled at us as she walked by and said goodnight. Leading the man by the hand, she led him down the hallway back to her bedroom and I heard the door lock. Tears quietly began running down my cheeks as the memories came flooding back to when I was a child. Mother always had a man around. Some were okay. Some were not. I could hear echos of the past whisper "danger". As I quietly began to cry, Chip held me and spoke softly to me that he was there and that it would be alright. I knew that as long as he was there I was safe. But he would have to go home soon leaving me with my fears and that man in the apartment. My heart began to beat faster as the fear crept in.

Chip continued to comfort me and held me close as we began to once again kiss. He ran his fingers softly through my hair as I naturally leaned towards him. Then he kissed me as he lay me back onto the sofa. We lay together quietly as he held me in his arms. I continued looking up into his trusting and loving eyes. Chip began to slowly kiss my lips; wiping tears from my face. I felt secure and truly loved for the first time in my life because I began to believe that I was his. Without words I understood that he required nothing from me. Nor would he ever force himself upon me. I knew that he wanted to be with me but only if I wanted him. I had so many firsts with Chip. I believe now it's because with him for the most part, I felt safe.

As we continued kissing, the passion within us took over once more. Laying as one, we found our rhythm and moved slowly in sync with one another as Chip lay over me as a protective covering. I could feel his heart beat; the hardening of his body upon mine as we melted into one another. With Chip, everything felt so right and natural. He continued kissing me passionately as we moved. I wanted more of him. For the first time in my life, I wanted to give myself to a man; to my Chip, exclusively. His body pressed heavily against mine and as I felt him, I began to softly moan.

However, my moaning triggered him. He knew we were within seconds of not being able to withhold ourselves from each other. Without warning, he stopped and pulled away from me again. As he sat up he closed his eyes momentarily. Chip began looking sternly into my eyes and it was frightened me. What did I do I wondered, to upset him?

"What's wrong?" I asked breathlessly.

"We need to stop. I need to stop! We can't do this Sarah Marie." He said.

With that, he stood up completely and took a deep breath. I just lay there looking up at him.

"I need to go home Sarah. I'm sorry." Chip seemed angry.

"Please Chip, don't go. Don't leave me. Please?" I pleaded quietly.

"Sarah, don't get me wrong. I want to be with you." He said as he took another deep breath. "But not like this." He turned; walking towards the door.

I quickly stood to my feet. "At least kiss me goodnight?" I couldn't help but smile as I innocently looked up at him.

Chip smiled and walked over to me. He cupped my face gently in his hands and gazing longingly into my eyes, quietly asked, "What am I going to do with you young lady?"

"Kiss me goodnight?" I replied teasingly. "Just one?"

Chip smiled from ear to ear and leaned over to kissed me one more time; deep and passionately. I could feel myself beginning to melt into his arms again. But he quickly pulled away and let go. Then, turned around and walked out the door; leaving both of us very frustrated. I already knew that it was going to be another very long, disparaging night of our love's desires not realized.

As I lay in bed alone, I gave into the fact that I was irrevocably in love with this man. What was I to do? I was leaving in a couple of days. I had a fiancé at home. Brandon couldn't hold a candle to Chip and I wanted to stay. But things never turned out the way I wanted.

I already knew that. If I stayed, Chip would most likely loose interest and move on; leaving me with mother. The only good thing as far as I was concerned about Texas "was" Chip. Other than him, I had no good memory to rest upon. I tossed and turned all night. Should I stay and take a chance on Chip? Should I give up and go home? This man had turned my world upside down and although I knew exactly what I wanted, I was afraid of being left once he came to know me.

My fears were driving me back to Georgia. I knew if I stayed and Chip grew tired of me or just changed his mind, I'd have to see him at the station from time to time. I would just be heart broken. Oh God, I'd be stuck living with my mother again! Never! I couldn't go through that again. Too many variables for me to consider staying. But what was I retuning to? A father that didn't approve of anything that I did and no one that I chose to date. Thus, my boyfriend Brandon in Georgia was the perfect one for irritating my father. Brandon was mean and enjoyed a good fight. He said that he loved me but was also was abusive both physically and emotionally to me. Soon, Brandon was leaving for the Army. That meant that if we married I would be out of my father's reach. He couldn't yell and tell me how stupid I was any more. Little did I realize that I was trading one for another just like my father.

The next morning I quickly dressed and headed to the station with mother with hopes of seeing Chip. We had one last day together. Chip had to work that night. It was horrible for us both. We would not have that one last night that we wanted so desperately together. We stayed on the phone that night talking while he worked and played music. Simon and Garfunkel began singing "Cecilia". I liked the song so much that Chip played it twice. I now wonder what I was thinking? Was I even thinking at all? As I look back at it, that was the worse song to drill in Chip's memory the night before I was to leave. The next morning I began to pack and get ready to go. Mother was not happy with me. She drove me to the airport in Abilene and I flew home back to Atlanta.

KTXS T.V. Station

Candace H. Hunt: my mother (head continuity writer)

Candace Marie Hunt 1972
AKA: Sarah King

Clyde E. ALY 1976
AKA: Chip Lowery

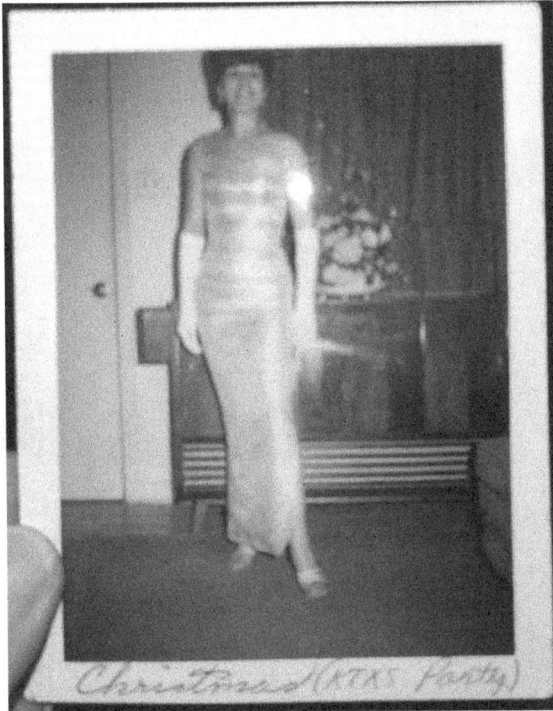

The Door (chapter 5)
Mother ready for the KTXS Christmas party

Mother at work.

Joe and Candy Wedding Day July 15, 2006

2019

**Clyde & Candy July 23, 2020
at KTXS T.V. Station
Abilene, Texas**

KTXS TV Station in Abilene Texas

Chapter 7

Welcome Back...Not So Much

MY FATHER PICKED ME UP at the Atlanta Airport. He could tell that my spirit was down.

"What's wrong with you?" He said gruffly.

"Nothing dad. Just tired." I sighed.

"Sarah Marie, you look like you've been crying. What's the matter with you?"

"Did you and your mother have another argument?" Dad asked.

I took a deep breath; nervously chewing on my lower lip. The last thing that I wanted to do was tell my dad about my week with Chip. I could play it all out in my head; dad making fun of me for having a new guy. I had so many boyfriends come and go. The expression that you have to kiss a lot of frogs to find your prince wasn't far from the truth. I had dated a lot of frogs. They all thought I was cute. I hated that word... cute. It made me sound like a pet. But when it came time in their minds to give myself up, I said no and they bolted. I didn't have to say no to Chip. I didn't want to say no to him. He was a gentleman. He controlled himself. Great; the one and only time I wanted to be with someone and he said no. What's wrong with that picture? Even a better question, what's wrong with me?

Then there was Brandon; my fiancé. Brandon was 6'3", brown eyes and thick mahogany hair touching his shoulders. He enjoyed a good fight and never lost one in school or otherwise. He was German with a lethal temper. He didn't drink or do drugs. He was mean all on his own. Brandon already suspected that I had been with another guy while visiting mother in Texas because he could never reach me when he called. I only spoke to him three times the whole week; upon arrival, by accident as I headed out the door, and a quick call early that last morning in Texas to let him know that I was on my way home. I couldn't even say I love you or I miss you. Yes, he knew something wasn't right.

I walked into the house where Mom greeted me with a big long hug. I needed that hug. She stepped back and saw the tears in my eyes and took me by the hand upstairs. Dad asked where we were going.

Mom said; "We'll be back George. I need to talk to Sarah for a moment." With that, we disappeared into my bedroom and sat down.

"Darling, what's wrong? " she asked. I just looked at her and burst into tears. She wrapped her arms around me and held me for a minute. Then she said, "Is it the new boy that you met at your mother's you told me about.. Chip?"

I nodded my head yes as the tears rolled down my cheeks. " I don't know what to do. This guy is different. I told you that he was twenty two; right?" Mom nodded.

"Mom, Chip is wonderful. Really! He's kind,..respectful, and treats me like I'm special. Like I'm important to him."

Mom smiled. She had the most peaceful understanding eyes and I could tell her anything. Somehow when she looked at me, I knew things would work out. "Darling, you are special and you are important."

I sort of smiled and said; " I am to you. I'm not to dad. Brandon thinks of me as a possession."

I shook my head as I stood up and began to pace back and forth in my room.

Mom stopped me and took my hand; "If this Chip is that wonderful, why did you come back? Maybe you should have stayed awhile longer to see if this is real or not."

I continued crying. " I'm afraid Mom. I'm afraid of Brandon being mad at me"... I paused.

"And what else?" Mom asked.

"I'm really afraid of Chip changing his mind. It would kill me inside if he gave up on me. I mean, he's so much older than me. I would have to change schools and live in Abilene again with mother. Mom, she's still bringing guys home. Nothing's changed."

"Your memories." I nodded my head yes. " Have the nightmares returned?"

I replied; "Yeah they have." Mom thought for a moment and asked; "Have you told your mother about those nightmares?"

I shook my head no. " Mom, Mother would not believe me if I told her. She would think that I was making it all up."

While we were talking the phone rang. It was Chip; making sure that I had made it home safely. We didn't speak long as I remember. I do remember hearing "I love you and I miss you." I told him that I loved and missed him and we hung up. I felt lost; out of place without Chip. Suddenly, I realized that I felt like half of me was missing. It was the oddest feeling. Hearing his voice was as if it had been a month instead of hours since I'd seen him last. I was so confused.

About that time, Brandon drove into the driveway. Part of me was glad to see him. I thought that I might feel better. He jumped out of his car and running up to me, he threw his arms around me and swung me around; lifting me off the ground. He kissed me. But it just wasn't Chip's kiss.

Brandon said," What's wrong with you Sarah? Aren't you glad to see me?"

I plastered a smile on my face and said of course! He asked me to go with him to his mother's house where he was living. But I declined and said that I was too tired. I even lied and said that I missed my mother. Brandon wasn't buying it. But, he left for the night and I stayed up in my room.

Chip called daily and I even received letters almost every day from him. It was killing me not to be there with him. Brandon picked me up the second day home and we went to his mother's house. As we stood in the front yard, Brandon stood before me and began asking questions. When he asked me what was going on, I knew this conversation wouldn't turn out well for me. "Why aren't you happy to be back?" His voice kept getting louder with each question. "What did you do all week? Why weren't you ever home when I called you?" Brandon had pulled out his swing blade; flipping it open and closed as he continued his inquisition concerning my week in Texas.

"Sarah, tell me what is going on with you!" He demanded.

I stood and said nothing.

"Sarah, did you meet someone else out there?"

I continued to say nothing but looked down to the ground.

"Sarah! HAVE YOU BEEN WITH ANYONE ELSE? ANSWER ME!"

I stood there beginning to feel fearful. Brandon was livid.

"Damn it Sarah, answer me!"

I looked him squarely in his eyes and timidly answered yes. With that, he suddenly threw his blade at me; calling me a few expletive names as it flew by close to my cheek and landing solidly into the tree that I stood beside. Half of me was scared to death. But the other side of me was unbelievably angry.

"Brandon! You almost hit my face!" I screamed.

"Sarah, if I had wanted to cut your face I would have!" He screamed back as he walked closer to me. We continued to argue and Brandon decided to take me home. I remember him driving like a mad man and yelling at me all the way. I was so glad to plant my feet on my own turf. Burning his tires, Brandon sped off in an explosion of anger.

The letters kept arriving. They were sweet as I recall. I missed Chip so much that I secretly planned another trip to Texas within a couple of weeks. One day just after the mail came, Brandon came to pick me up and take me to his mom's house again. We had been arguing daily since my return but I thought, maybe this time will be better. Mom handed me a letter that had just arrived from Chip. Because Brandon was driving up, I pushed it down into my purse for later. I jumped into the car and sped off. Brandon seemed to be in a better frame of mind.

We walked into his mom's house. After saying hello her, she went down to the basement to wash clothes. One of his sisters asked for gum so I pulled the gum out of my purse. Unfortunately for me, Chip's letter fell out. Brandon ran over and grabbed it before I could.

Looking at the name and address he demanded; " Who's Chip Lowery? Is this the guy you cheated on me with in Texas?" I just fearfully looked up at him. "IS IT? ANSWER ME! IS THIS THE S.O.B. YOU CHEATED ON ME WITH AT YOUR MOTHER'S?!!!" Brandon was becoming unhinged.

I stupidly yelled back; "Yes! That's my letter! Give it to me Brandon!"

Brandon tore open the letter from Chip. Sarcastically, he read the letter out loud. The more he read, the more enraged he became.

"I love you? If you love me like you say, Sarah, come back to me! "He misses your kisses?!" Brandon sarcastically screamed.

Fire was burning hot within Brandon. His eyes blazed with rage. He jerked me up and demanded that we talk. Running me over to the basement stairs, he grabbed my hair and lifted me off my feet. He could see the fear in my eyes; but he didn't care. Quickly, he pulled me down the twenty old rickety wooden steps to the basement.

I began to scream, "LET GO OF ME! YOU'RE HURTING ME! Brandon, LET GO!" With each step my back hit and scraped against the wood. It seemed to never end. At the bottom of the steps, Brandon's mom just stood to the side saying nothing as she looked on.

Brandon was so angry that he rushed out the basement door. I then ran up the basement stairs and quickly called mom. Mom came and picked me that day. I made up my mind to make solid plans to return to Texas. Chip's letters were so romantic. His calls were sweet. I had to talk to Mom and get her advice before I called Chip. I was determined to go but was I just running off heighten emotion or was this something more?

"Chip is really in love with me Mom!" I exclaimed. "Look at these bruises Brandon made on me! Chip would never treat me that way."

"I know. Brandon should have never done that. I can't believe that you actually told him about Chip. You know how he is. But what do you know about Chip? You haven't known him long enough to really determine if he's the one; or if he's abusive or not. Remember darling, there's more than one kind of abuse. Emotional can be just as bad. It's all bad."

"Mom, Brandon point blank got in my face asked me. You know I can't lie very well. Although... I did lie to Chip about how I really felt about leaving." I said as I hung my head.

"Sarah, what are you really afraid of?" Mom's question pierced my soul and I began to cry.

"Mom, everything!" I screamed as I burst into tears.

"I'm scared of staying here and losing a chance with Chip."

"I'm scared of staying in Texas. I hate that place. I hate the thought of being stuck with mother! Bad memories. It's like these dreams I've have."

Mom was quiet; then asked; "Are you still having the dreams?"

"Yes! It's like I'm in this dark room and the door opens. Someone, a man comes in and starts whispering to me in a soft deep voice." I shook my head and closed my eyes.

"I can't make out his face; but he's big. He lies down next to me. Then he whispers, " Be still. No Sarah. Be quiet. I won't hurt you. Just be still." My whole body shuttered.

"He does things to me mom; in the dream he.... does stuff. He creeps me out. I hate him!" I cried. " I hate him! Somehow I know that mother is in the other room. I can't breathe. I can't scream. I just close my eyes and go stiff. Then I wake up."

"Okay. Alright Sarah. It's not something you need to dwell on right now. You're safe here."

Years later I would discover that it was more than bad dreams. It was the suppressed memory of Ray Gonzales; one of mother's many boyfriends molesting me at the age of seven.

"What else are you afraid of?" Mom continued. "There's something else; isn't there?"

I looked into mom's teary eyes. I could see she cared. Mom had the most understanding eyes.

"Mom, what if Chip decides I'm not what he wants? What if he changes his mind and decides it's only infatuation or something? What if he sees someone else and wants her more or just gets tired of me? I'm really in love. In love Mom! You wouldn't be there. You know mother. She'd just say find another. There's plenty of fish in the sea. But for me, Chip is the only one." I threw my hands in the air in frustration and then began pacing the floor.

"You know I have a terrible temper. I can't cook good. I'm hyper. I love attention and am too lovey dovey. I'm emotional. Crap, my own English teacher finds my poetry melancholy. Can you believe she wrote that on my final? She thinks I'm a depressed person. I'm too emotional! Even dad says I wear my emotions on my sleeve. He hates that mom! Mom, why would anyone want to stay? I'm me! Once the new wears off, Chip will just leave me. I mean, that's what guys do."

Mom smiled. "I love who you are! That's the way God made you. You need to like who you are Sarah. There's nothing wrong with you darling that lots of love won't cure. I've always said that out of all our kids, you are the one that would make the best wife and mother."

"Yea me...." I replied. "I wish other people saw what you do in me. Heck, wish I had as much confidence in me as you do."

I lay in bed that night trying to figure out what I should do. I was exhausted but sleep didn't find me until the wee hours of the morning.

Chapter 8
The Battle In The Silence

"GOOD MORNING DARLING. I'VE BEEN thinking about your dilemma. I think you should go back." Mom said. "You need to find out for yourself what kind of young man this Chip is."

"Really?" I sat and thought about it for a minute. "Okay. But how do I explain it to dad? Or even worse…Brandon?"

"You leave your dad to me! As for Brandon…" mom paused… "break the news to him here."

Plans were made much to dad's chagrin. He thought I was nuts. Nothing new there I thought. Brandon was angry. After a heated argument, I broke off the engagement. He was furious but held it in for the most part at our house. I was breathing easier once he left.

I called Chip and told him that that I was flying back to see him and what flight I'd be on. Dad couldn't fly me into Abilene this time. Chip happily agreed to pick me up In Dallas at Love Field. He was thrilled. I was a nervous wreck. I packed and headed for the Atlanta Airport again. Chip didn't know that Brandon and I had broken off our engagement. I never told him. Nor did he know what went on and all that I had gone through in order to return to Abilene.

I was excited but so nervous throughout the flight; wondering what would happen. Chip greeted me with a huge smile on his face. I was glad to see him. He greeted me with "his" kiss. I was hoping that would calm my nerves. But alas, no. Chip surprised me as he looked lovingly into my eyes and said; "Marry me." I stepped back in shock and said, "No."

I thought, "WHAT?" I'm not ready for this. Suddenly I realized that we didn't know each other well enough at all for marriage. I was blown away by his proposal! Chip had been right about dating and getting to know one another. Now, he blurted out "Marry me!" He didn't want to discuss it. I couldn't explain my thoughts on the matter. He shut down emotionally. So we sort of joked around talking about silly things. But that was about the extent of our conversation.

As we traveled back to Abilene, I changed it up a bit and asked Chip if I could drive. At first he was hesitant.

"I don't know if that's a good idea Sarah."

"But I have my license. I can drive. Please?" I begged. "I promise I'm a good driver."

"Your mother might not approve of me letting you drive my car." He insisted.

"Ah, she won't care; Please....?" I remembered batting my eyes and smiling at Chip as I pleaded even more emphatically.

Finally, giving in, Chip pulled the car over to the side of the road and reluctantly got out of the driver's seat. I jumped in and began to drive. Apparently, I continued to scare him out of his wits for quite a few miles. When Chip couldn't take any more he convinced me to pull over and let him drive the rest of the way. He was correct in his assumption. Mother was not at all pleased that he allowed me behind the wheel.

For Chip, the rest of the week went black in his memory. For me, I remember Chip becoming aloof and busy. When I came to the station with mother, Chip was too busy to come see me. We went out a couple of times. We tried to talk but he was closed up. He barely kissed me goodnight when we did go out. We spoke on the phone a little. But he was cold and non responsive to anything I had to say.

Maybe I made a mistake; but I felt like he had only asked me to marry him out of desperation. Would he have resented me for that later? Suddenly, I was the clear headed one. I knew that I had hurt him. But I also knew that just prior to me leaving Abilene the first time, he only wanted to date me and see where it would go. That was iffy to me. But now, I realized that he was right. Our roles had become reversed.

The fears were driving me back to Georgia. Chip, I thought, had decided that he didn't want me. If I stayed and I was right or he just changed his mind about being with me, I'd have to see him at the station from time to time. I would just be heart broken. Oh God, I'd be stuck living with my mother again! Never! I couldn't go through that again. Too many variables for me to consider staying. Chip's lack of affection towards me helped to determine my decision to leave. I had no reason to stay any longer. There was no hope of being with Chip.

As I lay in bed night after night, thoughts of Chip circled around in my head. Chip acted as though we had never had anything at all between us. I wanted to run back to Georgia.

But what was I retuning to? A part of me felt boxed in. With Chip no longer wanting me, I felt as though I had no choice but to return to my home.

Daybreak finally arrived and I pulled myself out of bed. I was tired and had it not been for my desire to see Chip, I could have just stayed under the covers for the day. My mind was racing. What am I going to do? Back in Georgia I still had a so called boyfriend who sometimes was my fiancé; Brandon. I was not in love with him. I thought I loved him when I got on the plane to Texas the first time. But loving and being in love were two very different things. After having been around Chip all that first week, I wasn't sure I even liked Brandon. Brandon had that hot temper and mean streak a mile wide. The question that haunted my thoughts and fed my fear was, "What happens if I stayed in Texas and Chip really didn't want me?" How could I face that deep a heartbreak? The pain would be much deeper and getting over Chip could prove to be impossible. I was so confused. Did he even love me anymore?

Things weren't any better with mother. We argued all week. We argued over dad. She raked me over the coals concerning Chip. The week was a total bust. I cried a lot at night alone in the bed wishing Chip would come and make everything alright again between us. Nothing went according to plans.

Chip agreed to do mother the favor of driving me back to the airport in Dallas. It was a long silent drive. Once there, Chip began to ask me once again to stay. But why? He'd ignored me and was so cold all week. Why should I stay? He confused me. I didn't understand his sudden change of heart. I tried to have a regular conversation with him. I even joked around a bit but Chip was in no mood for keeping it light. I kept looking at him. But he would turn away from me. It was all I could do not to cry. I was desperate to understand his motives. I was baffled and just didn't understand his about face attitude.

Finally, the gate attendant called for boarding and I stood to my feet as I picked up my bag. I turned to say goodbye; holding my feelings for him at bay. My father had taught me well. You never cry in front of anyone. It's a sign of weakness and lack of self control my father would say. I wish now that I had cried. I wish now that I had followed what my heart was telling me; stay!

Chip began to weep again as he did the first time that I left ; begging me to stay. All week he displayed nothing but frigid attitude towards me and now this? I didn't know how much longer I could keep up the façade. Why was he suddenly crying? Yes, I wanted to go home; but not for the reasons that I gave Chip. I had to do something before I myself cried and my rouse was revealed. I didn't trust his love for me anymore and that in itself tortured me. I wanted to believe him but my fear of him leaving me after the way he had treated me all week gave me courage. So I looked straight into his eyes and said, "Stop crying. It won't change my mind. I have to go home to Georgia."

Mom was my safe place. I felt so empty deep inside; so lost, as if a part of me were dying as I stared down at the floor. Why? Had Chip really gotten embedded that deep into my soul in such a short period of time? My heart was so torn!

Chip looked at me through his tears and said, "I love you Sarah. I always will. " He then kissed me goodbye. I took one last long gaze into his crystal blue eyes. Then, taking a deep breath, I turned from him and walked away. For the second time, I wept all the way home; feeling that I might have lost the best man that had ever come into my life or ever would. Chip would later tell me that after I left, a lady asked him if I was his girlfriend. He said that he replied yes. But his heart was telling him, not anymore.

I boarded the plane. I barely remember the stewardess asking me if she could do anything to help me as my tears streamed down my face. All I could do was shake my head no and turn back towards the window and weep. I felt as though my heart and soul were being ripped apart.

The loss was so great! It hurt because I couldn't stand to see him cry. I ached because I had broken his heart. I realized as I sat there looking out the window of the plane, that I would never feel his arms around me or taste his kiss ever again. My fear had driven me away from the love of my life. I felt my heart break into pieces. I had no one else to blame because I knew that my heartbreak was of my own doing. This was one mistake that I would have to live with the rest of my life I thought.

I returned home and eventually married Brandon. That was the second biggest mistake of my life. Always in the back of my mind, there was Chip. I missed him and some nights wept silently lying next to Brandon; especially when we had had a violent argument. I even called Chip a couple of times from Newport News, Virginia where we lived. Once I called; begging Chip to come get me; only to have him refuse. I called Chip a few more times but eventually stopped calling. There was no use. I had made my bed and I had to lie in it.

Mother came out to visit us once while Brandon and I were still married. Mother wasn't a good wife but she knew men. She hated Brandon and although he was nice to her, she knew what kind of man he was. She could spot an abuser when she met one.

She didn't mind reminding me what an awful mistake I had made by not marrying Chip. I didn't need to hear that. I knew when I got on that plane a year and a half prior that I had screwed up. I knew the day I said 'I do' to Brandon, that I screwed up. In fact, pretty much daily I was reminded of how badly I had screwed up. But it hurt the most when I would hear Chip's voice on the phone. Bittersweet memories and sad goodbyes were always slapping me in the face. Not to mention, the arguments over Chip that popped up every so often between Brandon and me. Yea mother, I screwed up big time. My consequences were bruises and the breaking of anything that belonged to me when Brandon was angered.

Brandon and I divorced after two and a half years of tumultuous married life. After he informed me that he was going to kill me the day after he was discharged from the Army, I made plans to leave him and get a divorce.

Two and a half years passed. Another failed marriage and that fateful trip in 1977 that Chip made to Port Lavaca to tell me he chose another woman to marry. I threw my memories into Pandora's box and locked them tight. I had become cold and heartless to the best of my ability in order to survive this thing called life. Frankly, the only thing that I felt secure with was my 357 caliber weapon.

Even after returning to Georgia and starting over, thoughts of Chip would suddenly grip my heart out of nowhere. I would wonder where he was and if he was still married. Mother had told me that Chip married a beautiful Hispanic girl named Aliana the following month after coming to see me and that they were happy. Good for him, I thought. I still missed him after all those years. I figured that he had forgotten about me. All I was to him was a bad memory.

In 2009 I was laid off from my managerial job at DVR Properties. I was told that the Villa Rica Police Department was looking for volunteers. I had some contacts there and was soon given the position of a file clerk. Their files were in such disorder that they were in desperate need of organization. This was right up my alley and I so enjoyed putting them in order properly. One day while standing in the lobby of the police department, a gentleman by the name of Jack came in and needed information. He was from Texas. As we began to talk, we quickly realized that we had a common acquaintance.

Jack: "You lived in Texas? Where?"

"I lived in Abilene. My mother worked for KTXS T.V. as head continuity writer in the 70s." I answered.

"Seriously?" Jack replied. "I had a friend that worked there. His name was Chip Lowery."

My heart began to beat faster and I found myself trying to catch my breath. I hadn't heard that name in years.

I smiled and replied; " I knew Chip. We dated for a short time. Really nice guy. How is he? Is he still married?" I inquired.

"So you know Chip. It's a small world; isn't it?" Jack said with a grin. "Yea, he's still married. He's doing well."

I quickly got a piece of paper and pen from the officer on duty and wrote my phone number down and asked Jack to call him and give him my number.

"Maybe he could call and say hi.

It would be good to talk to him and catch up after all these years."

Jack nodded in agreement; then he and I said our goodbyes. I never received a call. I had supposed that Chip just didn't want to talk to me. It saddened me off and on; each time Jack's visit came to mind. As silly as it sounds, it was the closest I felt to Chip since 1977.

But it wasn't long afterwards that I had three young grandchildren suddenly living in our home along with my mother in law, and found little time to think. So life went on with only fleeting thoughts now and then of Chip and that "chance" encounter with his friend.

Sometimes I felt as though that meeting was by no accident. On the contrary, it was a sad reminder; a kick in the gut, of the love that I ran from so many years prior. Every time I went even a few months with no thought of Chip, an old love song like "Layla" would play on the radio instantly producing tears or someone would do something that reminded me of him. I never could quite forget that special time in the summer of 72.

However, when Chip contacted me again on my birthday in 2020 and our conversations continued, I realized that I had never completely left his thoughts all those years; nor his heart. Georgia was on his mind as he accepted jobs even as late as 2005 in Atlanta. His thoughts, although never coming to fruition, still drifted towards me. That spoke volumes as he disclosed that information one evening to me. Our timing just seemed to always be off; as if fate had immensely enjoyed playing our lives out like a cruel Shakespearean tragedy. Our paths in some way, shape, or form would cross but never at the right time or place. We loved and missed one another from afar it seemed.

Chapter 9
Conversations In The Dark

ONE NIGHT AFTER MY BIRTHDAY in February, we were talking on Messenger and Chip began writing; reminiscing about the first time he met me and took me out.

Chip wrote; "You were my Pixie! I just stood there watching the most beautiful girl who ever liked me. She was so full of life and she actually liked me. I stood amazed. But she moved so fast. I couldn't keep up."

"I moved too fast? Explain please." I replied.

"You still move faster than me...emotionally. I can't even describe how I felt about you. Your presence filled the room. I was breathless." He paused. "I've even wondered if I was just inflating the memories.... But I wasn't. You were my first love." Chip paused again then wrote;

"I loved you so much it hurt!"

My heart continued to melt with each word he wrote. All the memories poured in and nothing but love flowed out. Forty eight years and nothing had changed. I was still irrevocably in love with him. It felt as though we had stepped back in time. We could still talk as though we had never been apart for hours. My heart still pounded at just the sight of his name on messenger with the anticipation of hearing from him. With each sweet word I would find myself trying to catch my breath.

Oh God, I was in so much trouble! I loved my husband; Terry. It didn't matter whether we got along or not. However, Chip being back in my life gave me new drive. There was a new skip in my step. I felt like a teenager. I began to smile more and laugh over silly things. I looked forward to hearing from him nightly. If a thought of him came across my mind a huge smile would appear on my face. We were in sync; playing off each other; joking and goofing around like teenagers so many years ago. We realized that we had never let go of each another and had been connected strongly in our hearts for forty eight years. As Chip said one night, we were each other's other half. We laughed over the craziest things. We didn't care about the time. We just knew that we were finally back together as one heart. The distance didn't really matter. Once again, we fit as we always had.

However, with both of us loving the Lord, the conviction became too strong. I had to come to terms with the fact that I loved Terry. But, I was and had always been "in" love with Chip for forty eight years. I tried not to bring that into our conversations. I wasn't ready to let go.

"Um…what was the name of that movie you took me to?" I asked.

"Clockwork Orange." Chip replied apologetically.

I wrote back. "Are you kidding? Weirdest movie ever! I didn't like it. I felt very uncomfortable watching it."

"We'll explore the choice of movie later. Needless to say, I was very embarrassed."

"You know, you are amusing at times." Chip said.

"I'm glad that I amuse you." I wrote.

It reminded me of the movie Twilight. Edward said the same thing to Bell. I chuckled.

"BTW, I took you to that movie because the sports director at the station said he thought I would like it. I was so embarrassed that I took you. I was afraid that you wouldn't go out with me again." Chip wrote.

"Yea, did you notice how many times I either closed my eyes or turned my head? I wrote; remembering how embarrassed I felt sitting through it. "It left scars… I never had seen anything like that."

Chip replied; "Neither had I. It was awful. Am I forgiven for the movie!"

I was smiling as I wrote; "I wasn't mad. But you were so much older; a man. I was seventeen and you were twenty two. I felt insecure and not really knowing what to say. I forgave you that night. You got a kiss goodnight I believe."

"Yes, I did."😊 I bet Chip smiled as he wrote that!

"You know that every time I hear "Layla" I think of you? I considered that my song for you. In fact, any of the Moody Blues, Heart, Zeppelin, or Linda Ronstadt all remind me of you."

I had to shake my head. How unbelievably beautiful we naturally fit as one. The love that I'd had for Chip not only resurfaced but became so much stronger than I myself had fathomed it could ever be. The love had become too deep to pull away without ripping my heart out again. His love and attention would toss me into raging waves; overwhelming my senses. His voice would remind me of all the lonely nights and days of longing for him through out those forty eight years. His loving words filled my memories; awakening my desires as I remembered more and more of that precious, yet all too short time we had together in Abilene. He said that I had always been his go to girl.

One Friday night, as was our custom, we texted back and forth about meeting again. We dreamed of seeing each other again for the first time since 1977. Terry sat on the sofa next to me with his drink and headphones on listening to music and watching videos. Our conversations would show up on the tablet's screen and Terry ignored them. Who does that? It was odd. So as Chip and I would talk about our dreams, Terry just watched his videos.

We spoke of the what ifs of how it would be to finally see each other again face to face.

"I'm afraid that I might cry seeing you again." I wrote bluntly.

Chip wrote back; "Why, would that be bad? But I recognize how you think. I like how you think. You're my other half. I'm your other half."

"Getting inside my brain, my thinking can be a scary place to go… it scares me sometimes." I replied.

"Well I'm not afraid. Not of your thinking. I'm afraid of disappointing you." He wrote.

"Never. I know you. I may not know every detail. But I know your heart." I wrote to assure him.

"All I know is that I've been happier in the last couple of months since we started talking. I had forgotten that happiness. I'm coming out of my shell. I talk to people easier. I'm sleeping better and smiling for no reason. Just happy. My friends see it." He wrote.

"I'm glad that I make you happy. I need to go." 😮 That made me smile. I was so happy that I brought a smile and even laughter to his face.

"Goodnight Sarah. 😮 Goodnight Chip. 😮

One morning Chip woke up to a voice message that just said; "Good morning Love. Hope you have a wonderful day."

Chip texted back later: "Why are you so loving with me?"

I texted back: "You mean the world to me. I just want to make you happy for the day."

There was no reply for a moment or so. Then he thoughtfully replied:

"I've never made anyone happy like that. I've never done anything to make anyone happy like that. I really don't understand you at times. But I'm glad of it."

"Chip, you're my first love. You're back in my life. It's okay Chip. You're in Texas. You're part of me again. That makes me happy."

Chip replied; "Yes. Ditto"

We both were putting laughing emojis like two teenagers. We would laugh and joke around for days; weeks. Before long, it became months.

Chip texted one day; "I am learning to think of you as a blessing rather than an all or nothing situation. Is that how you feel?"

"Yes exactly. We can do only what we can do. My love transcends time and space Chip."

"For our love to last this long under these circumstances is amazing." He replied. "It's a love that can and has existed for forty eight years. I love the innocent girl that I used to know. She just didn't know how innocent she was."

"Chip, I only felt innocent with you. You were the first guy who only wanted to love me without anything in return. I fell in love with you because you saw me." I paused. "I'm sorry. Too much."

"I still do. You're a beautiful spirit. There's nothing to forgive." Chip texted.

"I just need to think about all this."

"Chip, I know that we can't keep this going. I'm so sorry. This is all my fault." I began to cry.

"Geez Babe, can't you see that this is not all your fault? I didn't ask you to get away. I just asked for some time. Don't run again!"

I left messenger panicking over the left turn that our conversation was headed. But then I saw his message.

Chip became even more emphatic. "Come back to me. I'm scared too! I know your heart. It's a good heart. So don't give up on it...or me."

I felt compelled to return and not leave him hanging.

"I am so in love with you but there's Terry. I love him. He's my husband. I just am so conflicted!" 😣

We continued for months writing back and forth. From time to time, we'd talk on the phone. Each time that we did, we laughed, joked around and sometimes argued about how to resolve the issue of my marriage. It was always a sticking point that neither of us could ignore.

Chip called me one morning and said; "We need to talk."

I knew that didn't sound good but I went ahead and said; "Okay. What is it?"

"Sarah, in all my years of being a Christian I've never heard the voice of God....until today."

I was almost afraid to ask. I had already been fighting with the Lord for weeks. I knew right from wrong. I knew what He wanted me to do. I just didn't want to turn lose.

"What did He say?" I asked.

"Sarah, He said; "You have to give her back to Me. I'm not done with her yet."

I began to cry.

"Sarah, please don't cry. I hate it when you cry. It hurts me too." Chip said. "You have more to lose than I do."

I told him that I had to hang up and that we could discuss the matter latter. "I love you Chip."

"I love you too." He replied.

It was a long morning. Thoughts were swirling in my head and aching in my heart.

That afternoon Chip wrote; "Here's the deal darlin'. I don't want to be the reason that you walk away from your old life. But if you do, let me know. I would like to see if we could put our lives together and live happily ever after. I am in love with you. If you walk away, I will miss you. I just don't want to hurt you anymore. I can't continue fighting with you and I can't be in the middle. With my heart,....."

"This is my way of giving you back to God. With my heart,"...... Chip.

"Please don't let me become just a distant memory." I pleaded. "Please don't forget me Chip."

Chip replied; "I couldn't even if I wanted to. You've been with me nearly fifty years."

We didn't have contact for about a week. It was killing both of us. I finally gave in and wrote;

"I miss you."

He wrote back and we began talking once again.

But the Lord wasn't having it. He spoke once again to Chip.

"Sarah, God keeps telling me that I have to give you back that He's not finished with you yet.

I got mad yesterday and told Him you deserved more than you've gotten. My hands were even fisted up. He just said that He would take care of you." I asked him; 'Well, what about me?'

He said that He'd take care of me too. 'My grace is sufficient.' I said; "Fine! But it's not her fault!" And that was the end of the conversation."

We said our goodbyes; again.

I called him. But Chip grew distant and cold towards me as we spoke. He finally said that he couldn't keep this up and didn't want to talk to me anymore.

"But you said that you were in love with me! That you needed me!" I cried.

"I'm sorry. I love you but I'm not in love with you. I thought I was. It's sort of like those two girls that I dated after you left. The first couple of months I was crazy about them but then lost interest. I have to admit, I was so enchanted with you when we first began talking. All the memories flooded in. But that's all it was; enchantment. I'm sorry. This is my fault. I'm sorry if I led you on. It wasn't my intention. I never meant to hurt you Sarah."

I sat there on the other end of the line speechless. My heart felt like it was going to burst within me. I never saw that coming.

"You have the nerve to compare the love that you said you had for me to those girls that you dated? You..." I paused. My mind was racing trying to remember all that he had said to me and about us over the last few months. Suddenly, I realized that I had never met this cold hearted man before.

"If something happened and I was free, would you come for me still?" I was reeling.

"I don't think I would even if you were free. I don't think we would be good together."

The cold hearted words broke me into. I was devastated; destroyed piece by piece with each hateful word that spewed out of his mouth. The lips that I had longed for to touch mine for over forty eight years had just razed me down to the ground. The same lips who had said he'd love me forever.

"You played me! Why? Did God really speak to you or did you just use Him to make your get away? You've been lying to me this whole time? Why didn't you just tell me at the beginning? Chip... answer me...you owe me that!" I pleaded.

But he was silent. Finally he said; "goodbye Sarah." With that, the phone went dead.

November was a cold hard month full of weeping silently into my pillow at night as I lay by Terry. During the day while alone, I wailed and yelled out to the Lord. My days and nights through December were hard and not a day without tears, anger, and sadness in no particular order. By the end of December I came to accept my life as it was. Terry had stopped drinking and we began to do more together; so things were better between us.

I still went back and forth with a range of emotions. They were unforgiving; a daily fight within would ensue. In the morning I would spend it just missing Chip; trying to hold my tears back. By nightfall I became angry; sometimes enraged over my stupidity for ever loving him. I couldn't kill the deep love that was buried inside. It chased me down in my dreams in the wee hours of the morning and sleep fled from me. But I had always been told that no matter what went on; this too would pass. I took solace in those words and longed for the day I could lock every word, every memory, away forever.

Christmas, New Years, and my birthday passed with only silence from Chip. My birthday was the hardest to endure. All the memories of that Super Bowl night would haunt me all day and tears flowed.

Chapter 10
Timing Is Everything

A PANDEMIC COVERED THE EARTH IN the first part of 2020; hitting the USA hard. Americans were ordered to shelter in place for months. The job loss was tremendous. Schools closed for the rest of the school year. Thousands died worldwide. I had planned a trip to Texas at the end of July to visit my family. But the Covid19, as the virus came to be known, lingered for two more years. It was early February of 2022 just after my birthday that Terry contracted the virus and died. We had barely finished building our house. It was a very sad time.

I planned another trip to Texas; possibly at the end of May in hopes of seeing my family as well as maybe reaching out to Chip. I tried calling him around Christmas two or three times to no avail. He wouldn't take my calls or answer any of my messages. When Terry came down with Covid19 at the beginning of February, I even messaged Chip requesting prayer for Terry. In my last message just two days before Terry died, I pleaded with him to call me. I really needed a friend because it looked like Terry wasn't going to make it. I never heard from him. Fifty years and he just walked away as though I meant nothing to him all. Inside I felt like a death had occurred already in my soul.

I had hoped that we could work things out so that we could at least be friends. I missed him terribly. At the same time, he really hurt me by not being there even as a friend when I needed him so. The horribly cold hearted things that he had said to me the last time we spoke, still stung. I felt like an idiot for missing him; for loving him still.

After Terry passed I could feel myself going numb inside. Every dream, every bit of love that I felt went numb. I wandered around the house finding things to do to keep myself busy. I couldn't help but wonder what the future held for me now. I decided to take each long and empty day one step at a time. I put one foot in front of the other and tried to remember to breath.

When Terry passed, my daughter Layla had asked me if she should call Chip. I said; "No; don't bother him. It's over. It's been over." But she phoned Chip anyway against my wishes to inform him that I was no longer married.

Two days later Layla confessed that she called Chip. I was furious when I found out that she had gone against my wishes. What Layla didn't know was that Chip decided to save her number in his phone.

"Did I not tell you; don't call him?!" I screamed. I was in tears. "Didn't I say don't bother giving him any information. He doesn't care? Don't you get it Layla? He doesn't love me anymore! I never want that name spoken around me ever again!"

"Ma, I'm sorry. I'm sorry! Please calm down. He was cold on the phone anyway. I had hoped that he would come see you. I'm so sorry. I believe you're right."

"Why do you say that? What did he say when you told him about Terry?" I asked.

My heart was pounding as I walked toward her. Layla peered down at the floor.

"What did he say Layla?" I demanded.

"Not much. Just thanked me for calling." Layla just hung her head. "I'm so sorry Ma."

I burst into tears. All this was too much! There had been a small part of me that still hoped Chip loved me when I found out that my daughter called him.

Terry and I had gotten into a good place in our marriage finally, in January before he passed; then I lost him. Chip appeared to be nothing more than a bittersweet memory now. Unbelievable! I thought; as I walked into my bedroom and closed the door. After fifty years and he just walked away. I lay across my bed and wept. My whole life had a taken a left turn in the twinkling of an eye. I didn't know which I ached over more; the loss of Terry or Chip at that moment. I just knew.... I felt utter emptiness inside my soul. Days passed and I tried busying myself doing projects on the property.

In mid March Layla received a phone call.

"'Layla, this is Chip. How are you?"

"I know who this is. What do you want?" Layla replied gruffly.

"How's your mother doing?" Chip asked.

"What? Your asking me that? All you had to do Chip, was answer the phone when she called and you'd know! Do you suddenly care or something?" Layla was steamed that he had the nerve to ask. "What the hell do you really want?"

"Layla, I care about your mother!" He replied. "How is Sarah Marie doing?"

"How the hell ya think she's doing? She just lost her husband and you were the other shoe that dropped. She'll make it through. She a strong woman; but it's gonna take some time. She's a hot mess right now."

Chip took a deep breath. "Layla, I want to come out to see her. She and I need to talk face to face. I need to explain some things to her. She needs to understand why I said what I did and why I didn't answer her calls or messages."

Layla laughed. "Like that's gonna happen! You just keep your old ass in Texas. That's where you belong. Mom has had enough on her plate without you coming out here screwing her up worse." Layla paused. Then she continued with her rant.

"Besides, what more is there to say? You said it all when you told her that you weren't in love with her anymore. You made it pretty damn clear how you felt when you called the love you said that you had for her earlier nothing more than... let's see... enchantment? Yes; mere enchantment! After all those times you told her that you loved her. Yea, dude, you've already explained yourself enough to mom. The last thing she needs right now is you telling her face to face 'again' that it was all mere enchantment. She is in no emotional state to be played. You're a real bastard! You know that?"

"That may be. But listen Layla, I want to work things out. We can now." Chip said.

"Dude, you really don't want to face her. She's not in a good frame of mind. She's liable to snap on you. You haven't seen that side of her face to face."

The frustration was clearly visible in his tone of voice. "I don't care. I need to see her and try and work it out with her."

"Just what exactly do you mean; work things out? You could have done that before if you cared." Layla snipped.

Chip chuckled. " You are you mother's daughter Layla; a powerful force to be reckoned with. Chip took a deep breath. "Look, I want to ask your mother to marry me. We're running on borrowed time. We've waited fifty years to be together and frankly until now, our timing has sucked. But we're both free to love one another now. I don't want to waste another day. But I need your help."

Layla sat there replaying his words that he said; wondering if he was lying or not, she said; "What do you want me to do?"

I'm flying out in three days to Atlanta. It would be good if you could pick me up from the airport and take me to her." Chip paused. "I've bought her an engagement ring in order to prove to her that I'm serious."

Layla laughed; "Good luck with that. Mom doesn't wear engagement rings. But...Um... okay. Send me your itinerary. I'll do it." Then she added; "I swear Chip, you make my mom cry again I'll shoot you myself. I carry a Glock. So don't you think for one damn minute I won't shoot you. It'll be worth going to prison for!"

"Geez Louise! Okay then." Chip hung up the phone shaking his head; wondering if he should even go to Georgia. But he had been waiting so long for Sarah that not even Layla's threats were going to stop him.

It was around 7pm when Layla drove up into my driveway. I had just come in from planting more day lilies on the side of the house and I was covered in dirt. My hair was in a messy bun on top of my head. I began realize that she had someone in the car with her. Could I have looked any worse? I thought. Shrugging my shoulders and taking a deep breath, I walked out onto the front porch as Layla jumped out of her car with a huge grin on her face. Her eyes were laughing. I could always tell when she was up to something because of her laughing eyes. They sparkled with glee.

Chapter 11
Surprise Visitor

THE PASSENGER SLOWLY GOT OUT from the other side. It was Chip. Under my breath I mumbled; "Just shoot me now....." All I wanted to do was crawl under a rock anywhere else but there and hide. After all the times I day dreamed of Chip seeing me for the first time in person, this look was not ever a thought. He had gotten a lot older with his thinning silver white hair. Time had not been very kind to either one of us I suppose. But through the wrinkles on his face I saw that unmistakable smirk and gleam in his baby blues. My heart began to beat faster and harder within my chest as he walked closer to where I stood on the porch. I knew beyond a shadow of a doubt; I was still deeply and hopelessly in love with this man.

Chip began to chuckle as though he had heard my thoughts. Dang, he could always read me so well. He didn't seem to care how disheveled I looked; him with his beguiling smile. He walked up, wrapped his arms around me and gave me a friendly kiss on the cheek. It was all I could do to keep my wits. My heart and mind darted back and forth between utter joy with the sight of him and the desire to knock him out. He still had power over my heart and he knew it. Darn that man! I had to laugh as I shook my head. Sixty seven years old and I felt like a stinking teenager; emotionally out of control again. He still had it going on. I knew that he saw it in my eyes. Seeing Chip again lifted my spirit; even if it was short lived. Then I began to wonder; why now? He had the nerve showing up here as if nothing had happened at all. After the mean things he had said last November, why come here now? So many questions running through my mind as to why he was here.

"Sarah Marie, you are a sight for sore eyes! I see my go to girl has been busy." He exclaimed with a grin as he looked around and then settling his eyes on my face.

"Chip, I'm filthy. My hair's a mess. And for the record, I'm not your go to girl! What are you doing here?" I was puzzled.

"You look perfect to me. I don't care. I've missed you. You're "my" Pixie now." He whispered.

When he said that I look perfect, it reminded me of one of my favorite songs for Chip and I; "Perfect" by Ed Sheeran. I found myself trying to catch my breath and slow my heartbeat as he spoke. Terry had only been gone for a little under a month. What do I do with Chip? I had a guest room but what would people say? Even worse, what would my kids and grandkids say if they knew that I had a man in my home that Terry built so soon after their grandpa's death? The reality was, I was grieving over Terry still; as well as feeling the guilt that I felt over Chip being a constant in my heart for all these years. I couldn't shake him no matter how hard I had tried…. My heart wouldn't let him go.

"Well, come on in. Have you eaten?" I asked. I shook my head and took a deep breath.

"Yup. Layla and I stopped on the way here and picked up some Chik Fil A. Brought you a large frosted lemonade. She said that it was your favorite drink."

I couldn't help but smile as he handed me the drink. I thanked him. Chip seemed so pleased with himself that he brought me my favorite drink. I grinned and continued to shake my head.

"Come on;" as I opened the screen door. "Welcome to my humble abode." I said.

As we all walked in, I gave Layla that right upper brow look as if I was not happy with her surprise. But Layla laughed out loud as she sat down at the table and said, "Unhuh… you know I did good." Then she winked. "Brat!" I mouthed silently. She just laughed that much harder. I knew that my feelings would be nothing but fodder for those two. They had at once become allies against me and teased relentlessly over my so called "rose colored glasses" outlook of the world.

I watched as Chip walked through the living room, eyeing the beautiful work that Terry had done throughout the open concept living room and kitchen area. Terry's gift was wood working but he was excellent in laying tile and.. come to find out, building a house as well. His handiwork was everywhere. Chip commented on how beautifully done everything was.

I thanked him and bragged on all the hard work that Terry had put into our home.

After dinner, we quickly cleaned up and Layla wiped off the table. I walked Chip from room to room showing off Terry's work around my home. He particularly liked my white china cabinet repurposed into a bathroom vanity with the deep green colored vessel sink in the guest bathroom.

"That's original. I've never seen anything like that. I like it!" He said as he opened the doors to the cabinet. "Sweet!"

"Thank you. It was my idea but Terry was always the implementer." I replied.

We walked out into the living room. Layla gave me a kiss goodnight and smiling at Chip, winked at him just before she walked quickly out the door. That left Chip and I in one long awkward moment of silence. He looked down at the floor with the all too familiar smirk on his face.

"Bring your things in here to the guest bedroom and get comfortable. I'll be back. I need a shower. So if you'll excuse me." I pardoned myself and quickly disappeared behind my bedroom door. This was not the how I wanted us to meet. I wasn't prepared. Everything felt off and I didn't know how to handle him being here so soon after I had buried Terry. We hadn't gotten to that old comfortable place where we had been before. Suspiciously I wondered what he was up to. Why; why is he here? I kept pondering that question as I showered and dressed.

I finished my shower and put my black slouchy pants that gathered at the ankles and a soft red short sleeved top on. I was too tired for makeup. I was doing good to get my hair dried and brushed. I thought back to all the care that I had taken back in the day to make sure I looked beautiful for him. But this evening I was too tired and just plain bewildered to care.

Chapter 12
Battle Royal

I RETURNED TO THE LIVING ROOM and Chip was sitting on the sofa waiting for me. I sort of felt bad for him. This was not the reunion that he had planned I'm sure. Where do we start? I wondered. His words back in November still pricked me as I thought back on our last conversation.

Me being me, I just sat down and looked him square in the eyes and asked once again; " Chip, why are you here? You made it very plain last November how you felt. You hurt me. You broke my heart and made me feel like a fool for ever loving you."

Chip's smile disappeared. "Go ahead. Get it all off your chest."

"You never mind about my chest or any other part of my body Mr. Lowery. What? You think after all your hatefulness you can…"

"Missy, you don't have to go all nuclear on me." He interrupted. "I wasn't hateful. I merely pointed out the truth as I saw it. You took it the wrong way."

Oh dear God, he had not seen nuclear yet. But he was fixing to!

"First of all, don't call me Missy. Second, you were a cold hearted…."

Chip interrupted. "Bastard? Go ahead. I said what I had to to push you back towards your husband."

"What's your excuse for not even being a friend to me when Terry was near death? What harm would have been done to show a little comfort?" I could feel my anger and pain rising to the surface. "You and your damn analytical mind. So it told you to say such hateful things to me? Like that was logical?"

Chip was beginning to show anger on his face. This was about to get ugly; real ugly. But at that moment I didn't really care. My pain was out and he needed to see it, as far as I was concerned.

"Don't tell me that it was ok to cheapen the love that we supposedly had for one another! Enchantment? I HATE THE USE OF THAT WORD CONCERNING OUR LOVE!" I stood to my feet; no longer wanting to be near him. "YOU SAID THAT YOU WEREN'T IN LOVE WITH ME ANYMORE ! SO, WHY ARE YOU HERE MR. LOWERY?" I demanded. " You said that even if I became a free woman you didn't think that you'd come out here! I'm not your type! REMEMBER?" I shouted with venom; looking straight at him as I backed away. "You get some kind of sadistic pleasure in hurting me more? Like you haven't DONE ENOUGH ALREADY?" I could feel the tears welling up in my eyes. " I broke your heart in '72 when I left. But you have more than gotten your pound of flesh between Port Lavaca and last November. WHY ARE YOU HERE CHIP?"

Chip stood to his feet and trying his best to remain calm. "We're both tired and I need to get in my ugly old box; as you call it, for the night. Let's try this again tomorrow morning."

"I'm sorry;" I replied sarcastically. "How rude of me. You can run. You're good at it!

"Well, I learned from the best!" Chip blasted.

"Go get ready for bed. I'm sure you're tired. I'll bring a hammer and some nails so you can NAIL THAT UGLY DAMN BOX OF YOURS SHUT FOR GOOD! Just make sure YOU'RE IN IT WHEN YOU DO!" With that, I quickly retreated to my bedroom and slammed the door; leaving him still standing there speechless in the living room alone.

Chip had never seen me like this. For the life of him, he could not understand my vicious anger towards him. After all, he had come all this way to see me and I wasn't giving him a chance to explain.

"She has got to be the most emotional girl that I've ever met." He mumbled to himself as he turned to go into the guest room shaking his head.

But then, he heard me crying. Chip never could stand to hear me cry. It broke his heart. He turned again and walked toward my bedroom door; pausing for minute, to decide whether to enter the tigress den or not.

I fell onto my bed and wailed. I didn't care if he heard me or not. I didn't care if the whole world heard me! I was so devastatingly heartbroken. I couldn't hold it in any longer. I hated the fact that I still loved him! I was as angry with myself as I was with him.

Just then, I heard my bedroom door open. Chip ventured in and walked over to me. He began to gently run his fingers through my hair just as he had done so many years ago. He laid down next to me; saying not a word. But began wiping my tears from my face. I looked up and he had tears running down his cheeks as well. He had that look of love beaming like a lighthouse shining into my dark sea of tears. He did love me! He did love me after all!

"Sarah, I didn't have the right to love you because you couldn't be mine to love. You were married. I didn't mean to hurt you. It was hard on me too; wanting you and knowing that I couldn't… shouldn't have you. You never left my thoughts or my heart darlin'. It made me crazy. I tried to explain it. But you took everything I said the wrong way. I can freely say now without guilt that I am and always will be in love with you. Please forgive me. That's why I'm here."

I moved closer to him and softly wept. "Do you really mean what you said?" I whispered.

Chip sat up and proceeded to pull a small black velvet box out of his pants pocket.

"Darlin', I'm here to ask you to marry me." With that, he opened the small box and there inside was a L'do'di ring. I gasped!

"Where did you find a wedding ring like this?" I was breathless with it's beauty.

"It's a wedding ring? I thought it was an engagement ring." Chip said with a puzzled expression. I had to laugh.

"But how did you find this?" I asked again.

"I Googled it!" He replied. "I found one of your Jewish sites that sold them."

"Wow! I'm impressed!" I laughed.

That all familiar smirk began to appear on his face. He knew that he had given me the perfect ring.

Chip had remembered me talking about how special a L'do'di ring was and what it meant to me. His ring was a beautiful 14 caret gold ring with the inscription on the outside that read, "A'ni l'do'di v'do'di'li" in Hebrew which came from the Song of Songs in the Bible. (I am my beloveds' and my beloved is mine.) The inside was inscribed 'To my Pixie. I'll always love you, Chip'. I smiled as he placed the ring on my finger. Then he kissed me. And there it was. His unforgettable delicious kiss. How I had longed for his lips touching mine!

We held each other through the night as we slept. Our souls finally reunited as one. We both had our first full night's sleep in years; much to our amazement. He hadn't taken his medicine and I never woke up once. Apparently, all we had been missing, all we had needed, was each other for a peaceful night's rest.

The next morning I went into my bathroom to freshen up and get dressed. Then walked out into the kitchen to make coffee while he did the same. It was a beautiful day as we walked out onto the porch with our coffee in hand. We were both at peace just being together. We had no need for words. We were no longer two halves. We were finally whole.

Chapter 13
Meet My Family

WE WERE DRINKING OUR SECOND cup of coffee when I heard the sound of a car coming up the gravel driveway. It was my oldest daughter Sandy and David, my grandson, driving up to the house. I whispered to Chip; "It's too early for drama and yet, drama has arrived. You may want your ring back after this visit." The peaceful smile left my face.

"Sarah, I'm not leaving. If I leave, I'm taking you with me." Chip replied sternly.

"Okay.... Just saying." I was concerned.

Sandy and David got out of the car and walked up to the steps; eyeing the strange man sitting on the porch next to me. It was 9 o'clock in the morning. I dreaded this visit. My grandson, David especially had a hot temper and I feared what might come out of his mouth. I had no idea how this visit would play out; but I was positive that it wouldn't be good.

"Good morning mother. Who's your friend?" Sandy said with a disapproving tone in her voice.

"Good morning. Sandy, David.. this is Chip Lowery; an old friend of mine. Chip, this is my oldest daughter Sandy and her son David."

Chip stood to his feet and put out his hand to shake their hand. "Yes. You're the one who took your mother for high tea on her birthday a few years back. I saw the photo of you two. I've seen yours too David. Pleasure to meet you." Chip said.

Sandy shook Chip's hand while her disapproval clearly shown on her face. I could tell that David had already made up his mind not to return the gesture. Chip sort of grinned and took his seat.

David began with his accusations; ignoring Chip's presence completely. He directed his questions to me.

"Grandpa hasn't been in the ground but about a month and you have a man in his house? Did he spend the night?"

"David, Chip flew in yesterday from Texas and yes, he spent the night."

"Where did he sleep?" David continued with his third degree.

"That's none of your business David." I replied nonchalantly.

Sandy chimed in. "Where did he sleep mother? He slept in the guest bedroom; right?"

Chip was shocked with all their pointed questions. He wasn't raised to be so disrespectful to his elders. Taking a deep breath I replied, "No."

"Mother!" Sandy exclaimed. David began interrupting his mother as he stepped forward toward Chip. "Did you sleep with him?" David roared. His hands were already balled up in a fist at his side.

I knew things were going to get ugly really quick. I stood to my feet and stepped forward toward them as Chip looked on in bewilderment as to what was going on. He stood also next to me.

"You stop right there!" I demanded. "Number one, yes he slept on my bed with me and two, no…we did not have sex. But even if we had, that's none of your concern. Chip is my guest and if you can't behave in a polite manner, you need to go NOW! I am sixty seven years old and I don't have to answer to you or anyone else in this family. Stop trying to control me. I will do as I see fit. You people do it daily; not caring if I approve or not. So keep your stones to yourself! I've known this man (pointing to Chip) for fifty years now. He's a good and honorable man. And I'll tell you another thing. I've been IN love with him since 1972. Now you go on and clean up your own back yards and leave mine alone! You got that?!"

Sandy said nothing except, "Let's go David. I love ya mom." She could see my anger was rising and wanted no part of it.

"Love you." I called back. David saw my determination to stand my ground and backed up. They walked back to the car.

With that, I took Chip's hand and we walked inside locking the door. I gave one last stern stare at both Sandy and David ; turned around, and went into the kitchen with Chip. They hastily sped off.

"Hum… that went well." I mused.

Chip was puzzled. "How do you get well out of all that? Cause darlin', I didn't see that at all."

"You didn't get jumped." I replied. "You're still in one piece; aren't you?"

"Geez Sarah Marie! Seriously?" Chip seemed still in shock over their behavior; especially David's.

"We need to take a ride. You still haven't met my youngest daughter; Candace." I said as I picked up my car keys.

"Do I want to meet your youngest daughter Candace?" Chip asked with a concerned look on his face.

"Well, it could go either way with her." I thoughtfully replied; rolling my eyes. "With my crew you never know."

"Can't wait…" he said. I saw the concern on his face. Frankly, I was concerned myself.

As we got into the car, I decided to phone Candace to let her know that we were coming to her house in Villa Rica.

"Hi babe. Do you you mind if I come over? I have someone important that I want you to meet."

Candace chuckled. "It wouldn't happen to be that guy from Texas would it?"

"Um… yes it is. How did you know?" I laughed.

"Sandy called. Do I need to say more?" She laughed. "Boy mom, you do know how to start a day with a bang!"

"Sorry kiddo. See you in a few. Love you babe." I said.

"Love you mama. Bye" Candace replied.

Chip breathed a sigh of relief as he gently took my hand and kissed it. He continued to look out the window at all the trees. We drove up to Candace's house. She was sitting on her porch waiting for us. As we got out of the car, She walked out to meet us with a huge smile; shaking her head as we walked up. I began to laugh. I knew that she had figured it out.

"Hi, I'm Candace but you can call me Candy. You must be Chip." She said.

"Yes. It's a pleasure to meet you Candy." Chip replied.

"Mom, this is the guy that you wrote about in your story; right?" She already knew the answer.

"Yea, this is the guy." I chuckled.

"So, what's the plan Chip? How long are you going to be here?" Candace inquired.

Chip burst into laughter. "I'll say this Sarah; I've never met a more lively group of family members in my life. They don't beat around the bush."

Candace laughed. "We get that from our mama."

"Yup. I know that's right!" Chip said with his smirky grin.

Chip lifted up my left hand to show the ring he gave me. Candace was delighted!

"We haven't worked out all the details yet. But the plan is," He continued. "I'm gonna marry your mother as soon as possible. We're not exactly spring chickens." Then we all laughed.

"We need to go. Thank you Candace for being so welcoming with Chip." I gave her a hug and we got back into the car and left for my house in Carrollton.

As we returned, my mind was spinning with questions as to what needed to be done before I could start my life with Chip. I felt an inner impatience and if left up to me, I'd leave it all and fly back with him when he left for Texas. The one thing that I did need was Terry's death certificate so that we could get married. I had convinced myself by the time we drove up the driveway that I could do it. I'd just leave it all behind. But still, I had to have that death certificate to legally become Chip's wife.

Chip and I slept on the same bed for the remainder of his visit; yet saving ourselves for our honeymoon. We held each other until falling asleep each night. It was the best sleep that either of us had in years. That is, until the last night before he boarded the plane for Dallas. That night was a hard one. At our age, we realized that each day was a precious gift from God.

We both wept at the airport holding one another. I tried to take in the memory of each and every touch. Every kiss and loving gaze of his eyes became more valuable as time quickly passed and they called for boarding. As he disappeared down the walkway toward the gate I prayed that God would keep Chip safe while we were apart. I hated that I wasn't going with him. So many years of wasted time apart gave me such a sense of urgency. Life was so short and I wanted with all my heart, to spend the rest of what little time I had left with Chip.

I waited impatiently for Terry's death certificate to come in from the state. Another week passed and the call finally came from the funeral home that the certificate was there. I jumped in my car and sped to pick it up.

I phoned Chip and gleefully shared my good news.

"Oh baby, oh baby! Get your cute Georgia butt down here girl!" He shouted.

"Just as quick as I can get a flight. I'll call you with the itinerary; ok?" I giggled.

"I love you Sarah Marie."

"I love you too. See you soon; Lord willing." I replied.

After making the arrangements to fly out the next day, I called Layla and asked her to take me to the airport. She came and spent the night with me at the house. We laughed and joked around till almost eleven. It was all I could do to close my eyes that night. The excitement over being not only Chip's wife, but finally making love with him was almost too much to allow sleep. I lay there smiling one minute and giggling the next. All our hopes and dreams were being realized at last. When I awoke the next morning, all I felt was joy!

Chapter 14

A Broken Heart

I COULD HARDLY WAIT TO DEPLANE and rush into Chip's waiting arms. But when I arrived at the baggage claim area, there was no sign of Chip. A stranger began calling my name. As he walked up to me he said, "Sarah, I'm Mack; Chip's friend. I'm here to pick you up. Chip couldn't come."

I knew that it couldn't be good if his best friend was here instead of Chip. Mack was only supposed to contact me if something had happened to Chip.

"What's happened? Is Chip alright? Please, tell me he's okay." I pleaded.

Mack sighed and said; "I'll tell you everything in the car. Let's go."

We finally left the Dallas airport on our way to Odessa. Mack began to explain what happened.

"We were on a shoot in Midland. Suddenly Chip grabbed his chest and collapsed." Mack shook his head in disbelief. " I never thought it could happen to him. I mean, I know we're not spring chickens anymore. But I never expected Ole Chip to ...."

"Mack, is Chip dead?" I took a deep breath. "Please Mack, just tell me!" I pleaded.

"No. He's still alive but his breathing is labored. They have him on a ventilator for now." Mack said with a groan.

"Thank God." I replied as I breathed a sigh of relief. "Mack, I'm so sorry. I know you are his best friend. This is hurting you too." I wiped my tears.

"Yeah, we've been friends for so long. I hate this for him...I hate for me too. He's a great guy. I'd hate to lose him." Mack thoughtfully paused. "Sarah, I think I hate this most of all for you two as a couple. You guys have waited so long! I've never seen Chip this happy. You're the reason, Sarah. Maybe I shouldn't say this; but he sure was looking forward to the honeymoon."

I smiled. "Me too Mack...me too. He's my Prince Charming."

"Well, I don't see it." He chuckled. "But I'm glad you do. You're his .... 'Go to girl.' I think that's what he calls you." Mack paused for a moment. "Or his Pixie. Yeah, that's the other one; Pixie."

"Yes. I'm that girl. I've always been his." I replied while staring back out the window trying to hold it together. We remained silent for awhile after that.

"Mack, is it totally hopeless? Is there nothing the doctors can do? I mean, there's got to be something they can do!" I cried.

Mack thought a minute. "Well, the doc did say there was an operation that could replace his valve or something ; but it's awful risky at his age. They said chances of him surviving are slim to none. His son didn't want to risk it."

"What did Chip have to say about it?" I asked.

"That's just it. He's not regained consciousness yet." Mack replied.

"I've got to see him! Maybe my voice will help bring him around. He should be the one to make that decision!" From that point on, determination was my middle name. I had heard that Chip's son was a force to be reckoned with. But his son had not yet met this force of nature!

We had to pass Abilene on our way. Abilene brought back so many memories of my life with mother, most of which I would rather not recall. But as we passed near the TV station, I thought back to the day I met Chip. He was like a sweet dream you have in the night. He had a broad smile that seem to light up a room. His laughter brightened my day and those crystal blue eyes of his, wow!

I thought back to the first time he really kissed me and the softness of his touch as he brushed his lips against mine. I remembered the passion that we shared. I smiled as I remembered the afternoon he caught me by surprise in the company break room at the station. He came from behind me; and whirling me around, he kissed me with such passion that I thought I'd melt right there. The hard part was walking back into mother's office with an uncontrollable huge grin on my face. All mother said was; "You must have seen Chip." Then she laughed. If only she had known! Boy, did I ever see him!

With the smile still on my face I accidentally blurted out, "WOW!" Mack turned to look at me. He saw the huge smile on my face and thought he'd better just leave me with my pleasant thoughts. Above all, I remembered Chip's deep love for me. So many memories ran through my mind as we drove on to Odessa.

I could sit and listen to him for hours talk about anything. I didn't care what the subject was. Even all these years later, I still loved to listen to him talk and joke around. He made me laugh. As old as we were, we could still go on for hours like two teenagers on the phone or text. Chip had become the brightest spot in my day.

To get my mind off the hard hitting realities, I wiped my eyes and asked Mack to stop and I offered to buy us a drink. As we returned to his car, I continued staring out the passenger's side of the window, quietly wiping the tears from my eyes. I asked God to please let me be in time. After all these years.... now this. I shook my head in disbelief. How cruel fate could be! With three more hours before we would arrived in Odessa, it seemed like it was taking forever to get there to my Chip.

When I awakened that morning I was so happy. Now, just hours later, the bottom had fallen out of all my years of hopes and dreams. I was finally righting a wrong and becoming Chip's wife. My emotions were all over the place. I also felt anger because of the strong possibility that there would be no future with him now because of his heart attack. It was as if I had been hit by a speeding fast ball right in the gut. Like water, everything was slipping through our fingers. I just had to get to him. Would fate truly be that cruel to us? It had been before. "No Sarah! Snap out of it! You'll make it in time. Stop the negativity; you have to believe. You just have to;" I continued telling myself and praying that God would bring him to while he was still alive.

Mack finally turned on the radio to kill the silence. He, like Chip, loved classic rock. I'm glad. I couldn't have handled the country and western with the heartbreak that those songs seem to bring. I had always wondered how people did it without medication for depression. The rock music actually helped with my brooding thoughts that chaotically swirled around in my head. Heart, Led Zeppelin, Stones and the Beatles played along with so many others. Memories were kept at bay as we drove into the outskirts of Odessa. But suddenly, as if on queue, saved for that very moment, Derrick and the Dominos began to sing "Layla". I burst into tears uncontrollably. Mack was at a loss as to what was wrong. Now what was he to do with a hysterically crying woman in his car? Finally, he turned off the radio and pulled into a parking lot.

"Hey, are you ok? What just happened?" I continued to cry. "Is there anything I can do?" He pleaded. I shook my head no. "Do we need to stop?" Mack was becoming desperate to fix me. There was no fixing. My heart was breaking into a million pieces; reminding me of my costly mistake and the wasted years we spent apart as a consequence of my running.

"I'm sorry! Layla was Chip's song for me."

Mack nodded in agreement and said, "I'm sorry. He did tell me that years ago. I had forgotten. I'm so sorry Sarah."

I felt bad for Mack. He pulled into the road and began stepping up the speed. He probably needed to escape the emotionally charged drama taking place in his car. Being a man, he realized at that point, there was no way to help except get me to Chip as fast as he could.

We finally arrived at the hospital just as the sun was beginning to set. When Mack's car came to a stop, I quickly jumped out and ran up the steps. I paused at the door and gathered my wits. As I looked around, I spotted the elevator and took it up to ICU.

I began my walk toward the waiting room. We would have our reunion as promised. Till death do us part would play it's role; but there was a possibility it wouldn't be as planned. It seemed as though it never went as planned. But I refused to believe that this was going to be our end. We had been through so much to get to this point that I just couldn't bare it ending; not like this!

As I entered the room, I saw him laying in his bed. Chip was still unconscious. His son spoke quietly with Mack explaining that I was "that girl." I could see his son's face become more serious as they spoke. Although I wondered what they were saying, I knew that I had to focus in on waking up Chip.

I gently began to whisper in his ear. "Chip, it's Sarah. I'm here and I need to talk to you. I love you and I need you in my life." I pleaded as I squeezed his hand. "Maybe I'm being selfish, but you promised me a honeymoon. You owe me!" Wiping the tears from my eyes, I continued to whisper. "Hey, we need to get you awake. If you don't wake up how can we fight and kiss and... make love for the first time? I've been waiting on this for fifty years! Chip, I love you. Wake up! Talk to me! You can't just lie there and sleep all day. I didn't come all the way from Atlanta just to watch you sleep. You know you snore; right?"

Chip squeezed my hand and opened his eyes. We called for the nurse and she came immediately. After the breathing tube was removed, Chip looked up at me and mumbled,

"No I don't." And there it was; the smirk.

"Hey girl. About time you got here. I've missed you.." Chip mumbled. I leaned in close and kissed him on the cheek. "I've longed to see you Love. I'm here now and will not leave you." I whispered softly.

"Our timing still sucks Sarah Marie. But you're still my go to girl.... always." He said with a slight smile. "You're here and that's all that counts."

The doctor was called to inform him that his patient was awake. His cardiologist entered the room and examined him.

Chip looked up at the doctor. "Well, how am I doing doc?"

"Mr. Lowery, you have a heart valve that doesn't work anymore; to put it simply. You need a replacement valve. The thing is, the odds are not in your favor of you surviving the operation at your age with some of the other health issues that you have. You only have a 15% survival rate." The doctor said. "I want you to think about whether this operation is something you really want to do. You can give me your answer when I make my morning rounds; ok? Do you have any questions that you'd like to ask me before I go?"

Chip nodded. "Yes I have one. If I don't take a chance and have the operation, won't I die anyway?"

"Yes." The doctor replied.

"So, if I have it and make it through, how long would it give me?" Chip asked.

"Ten or more years." Replied the doctor. Then he added; "if you take care of yourself and follow my instructions."

Chip looked at me and smiled; then said, "Let's do it!"

"Mr. Lowery, are you sure?" The doctor asked.

"Yup, I'm sure." Chip said with a slight grin.

"Alright, I'll check to see when there is an operating room available and assemble my staff. I'll get back to you as soon as possible." With that, he left the room.

Mitch, Chip's son was not pleased at all. "Dad, what if you don't make it through surgery? You really need to think this through."

"Son, I know the danger. But I also know that if I don't have it, I'm not long for this world. I still have living to do. I'd rather take a chance and maybe have the extra time."

Mitch stormed out of the room. Mack followed after him; hopefully to help him see that Chip was right.

"Come here woman!" I went closer to Chip's bedside as he gently put his arm around my waist and pulled me close. "Sarah, you okay with this?" Chip asked.

"Whatever you decide. When you make it through, we'll marry and have that honeymoon you told Mack you were looking forward to." I chuckled, blushing somewhat.

"You bet your sweet Georgia ass!" He weakly laughed. I just smiled and shook my head.

"Me too." I replied with a smile.

"Don't go all blushing bride on me. You know you want me!" Smirking all the way.

"I do my love; I do!" I burst out in laughter.

Mack came strolling into the room. "Hey dude, don't worry. Mitch will be okay. He just needs time to adjust."

"Thanks Mack." Chip replied.

I turned to leave for coffee and asked if Mack wanted some. He declined. So I left on a coffee run.

"Mack, find the Chaplain. I need to talk to him. I will need you later maybe for a witness.""

"Sure Chip." Mack left the room. Thirty minutes later Mack returned with the chaplain.

The chaplain asked Chip how he could be of service to him.

"Can you perform a wedding ceremony today?" Chip asked.

"I can if you have a marriage license. Do you have one?"

"No. But I need it done today before my surgery." Chip said.

I walked in just in time to hear the chaplain.

The chaplain thought a moment. "Mr. Lowery, I can perform what is called a Commitment ceremony. I just can't add that you're man and wife. That's the only legal thing I can do. Then, after you get out of the hospital, you and your bride to be can go to the courthouse and show them your Commitment Ceremony certificate and they will issue the license and make it legal."

Chip thought a moment he looked up at me and asked; " Will that do for now?"

"Anything you want to do is fine with me. You know that."

"Okay, it's settled. Let's do this!" Raising his voice in triumph.

Mitch walked back into his dad's room just in time to hear Chip's words.

"Do what dad?"

"Sarah and I are having a Commitment ceremony today before surgery. We will get married legally just as soon as I can get out of this place. You gonna be okay with that son? Time's a wasting and I'm not gettin' any younger."

"Whatever makes you happy dad." Mitch said with a smile.

"Good. Thank you son. I wanted your support. It means a lot to me. I love you. I love your mother. I always will. You know that; right?"

"Dad, I know. But I do want you to be happy. If Sarah does that for you, then do what you need to do."

The chaplain began; "Chip, take Sarah's hand and repeat after me. Chip Lowery, do you commit to love and cherish Sarah King?"

Chip looked up at me and said, "I Chip Lowery commit to love and cherish Sarah "Marie" King."

"Do you promise to keep yourself only for her until death do you part?"

"I promise to keep myself only for her until death do us part." Chip smiled.

The chaplain turned his attention to me and said, "Sarah King do you commit to Chip Lowery to love and cherish him?"

"I Sarah King do commit to love and cherish Chip Lowery and I also promise to keep myself only for him until death do us part." I became very serious; setting my eyes sternly on Chip and said, "You will not die on me today!" I squeezed his hand as I spoke.

Chip smiled and said, "Yes ma'am. But you know that none of us get out of this ..."

"Chip Lowery, don't even go there with me today or we're gonna fight!" I snapped back with tears in my eyes.

"Okay! Geez, you are the most emotional girl I've ever met! I was just kidding." Chip took a deep breath.

"If you two are through fighting, By the power vested in me, I pronounce you committed to becoming husband and wife." The chaplain smiled.

"Hey woman, get your Texas butt closer so I can kiss ya." Chip laughed. "You're mine now."

I bent down thinking that he was going to give me a soft peck on my lips. Chip had other ideas. He gave me a full blown Chip kiss and I melted right into his arms. Sick and in the hospital, that man still had it going on and I still could not resist. It was in his kiss.

The Cardiologist walked into the room and proceeded to tell us everything that would take place. "They will be in to take you down in thirty minutes. Are you ready Mr. Lowery?"

"Hell yes!" Chip replied. "Let's get this over with. I have a honeymoon to get to."

The cardiologist looked stunned! "Mr. Lowery, it will be four to six weeks before you can have sex. It could kill you otherwise."

Chip's expression changed. "Yea, but what a way to go!" He burst into laughter.

"Chip Lowery, what am I gonna do with you!" I exclaimed.

"Anything you want darling." He smirked.

Mr. Lowery, we will discuss this matter "after" your surgery." With that, he walked out of the room. The whole room burst into laughter. I don't know who laughed harder, Chip or Mack.

Thirty minutes passed quickly and with one quick touch of our lips he was gone. We had been advised that the surgery would last anywhere from two to four hours. By hour six, I was pleading with the Lord to let Chip live. Our fate had been so unkind up to this point. We were so close to finally being together. I paced and prayed.

The surgical nurse appeared at the door. "Well folks, it was a close call. He needed two of his arteries unblocked as well as the valve replacement. Mr. Lowery is in recovery and if he does well over the next two hours, he should be back here by four am. I suggest you go eat some breakfast. It's going to be awhile."

"May I see him just for a minute?" I asked.

"Come on. I'll prep you so that you can go in. I heard that you got married today."

"Well, more like betrothed." I said. " The only thing he could do was perform a Commitment ceremony."

"Huh. I have never heard of that before. But, whatever works." She said. " How long have you known each other?" She asked.

I chuckled. "We met in 1972 and dated and fell in love. I was only seventeen and couldn't handle it. So I ran. We continued to connect off and on through the years."

"And it's taken you two this long to finally pull it together?" The nurse seemed astonished that we had loved each other for that many years. She wasn't the only one.

I scrubbed my hands and arms and put the scrubs on that the nurse had given me. As I walked in I saw Chip lying unconscious. I sat down beside his bed gently took his hand kissing it and told him quietly that I loved him. After awhile, I returned to the visitors' waiting room to wait with Mack and Mitch. A few hours later Chip was brought back to the room groggy but awake. Over the next two weeks he improved quickly and finally was released from the hospital.

Once home, Chip relentlessly worked on his recovery. The doctor said that he could have sex once he could climb either two flights of stairs or walk a half of mile. Chip practiced that half mile walk daily. In the mean time we were legally married. One day he walked in with a huge smile on his face. I looked up from washing dishes just in time to see him raise both hands in a fist in triumph!

"I did it! I walked a half of mile.!" He shouted with robustly laughter. I shook my head and burst into laughter as Chip walked over and put his arms around me. Suddenly, I felt nervous as though I were a virgin bride. I could feel myself blushing and my face began to turn red. Chip stepped back a bit surprised.

"Sarah Marie! Are you actually blushing? I'll be gentle; I promise." He said with a huge grin.

"Chip, what if ...?"

Chip interrupted. "Darling, come with me." Chip led me down the hallway and stopped. He turned to me and gently brushed his lips against mine. Chip gazed into my eyes and brushed his lips again against mine a second time. Then he smiled sweetly; wrapping his arms around me.

"Sarah, I've dreamed of this moment for so long." Chip said with a smile. "You could never disappoint me."

We began walking into the bedroom as my heart raced on. Chip slowly ran his hands gently down the form of my body as I stood trembling with his touch. How old was I? I certainly wasn't that seventeen year old girl who once melted into his arms. But it sure felt like! But it sure felt like it! I was amazed that after all these years he still could render me joyfully surrendered to his love. With each touch, the sensations of electricity surged throughout my body and I melted into his arms just like I did at seventeen. As he began to unbutton my blouse I became breathless. The only thing I wanted, that I ever wanted, was to be one with him. He stood up at the edge of the bed and began to unbutton his shirt. I watched intently as he took off his clothes. I have to admit that I felt shy with Chip seeing my body for the first time. I tried to cover myself with my hands but he moved them away and softly said, "You're so beautiful. Don't ever try to hide yourself from me. You're beautiful darlin'." We lay skin to skin that night exploring each other's body making love; I never had felt so content; so complete. I wanted to lay in his arms forever. I had always heard that home was not a place but a person. I knew at that moment that I had truly found my home in Chip.

Each time we've made love it feels like the first time. As I have became more comfortable with my own body, my favorite thing to do is to tease Chip with that "come hither" look then disappear. He laughs and chases me knowing full well I'll let him catch me. Each time I touch his body I'm amazed at how much I still enjoy him. I love the scent of his skin as he wraps himself around me; tackling me to the bed or sofa. We love to to laugh and take trips to new places. But our favorite times have always been skin touching skin; laying in each other's arms and talking after making love. We're not spring chickens, as Chip would say. I'm amazed that we haven't broken something. But we have an enduring love that will last for the rest of our lives. Who could ask for more?

That was the last entry in mom's journal. She and Chip had a wonderful life together for twelve years. They both passed away the same night. Frankly, I'm not surprised that they were found holding one another with a slight smile on their faces. If Mom had written this, she wouldn't have called them smiles. She would have called them smirks. Layla

THE END

Candy Marie born Candace Marie Hunt in Norfolk, Virginia. Her happiest childhood memories were that of England where her father was stationed as a Navy pilot.

After returning to the USA, her mother moved to Abilene, Texas where they lived off and on until she was twelve. Candy's Senior year was at Pebblebrook High School in Mableton, Georgia while living with her father and step mother she lovingly refers to as Mom.

She and her husband along with their children lived in Guatemala and Israel as missionaries. While Co-founder of Jayim Israel Ministries in Guatemala, Candy Marie co-authored "Christians Celebrate The Biblical Feasts". She taught at Christian Academy of Guatemala for two years with a curriculum which she developed entitled "Recent Israeli History" and Hebrew 1#. Candy also tutored the twin sons of the Israeli Ambassador to Guatemala almost two years. Candy has been published in Villa Rican newspaper and Jerusalem Post.